The
Christmas
Promise

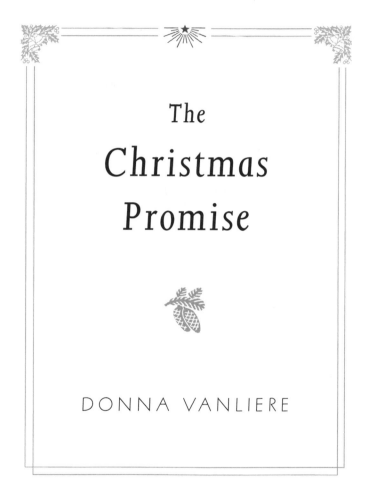

The
Christmas
Promise

DONNA VANLIERE

ST. MARTIN'S PRESS
NEW YORK

This is a work of fiction. All of the characters, organizations, and events portrayed in this novel are either products of the author's imagination or are used fictitiously.

Design by Susan Walsh

Library of Congress Cataloging-in-Publication Data

VanLiere, Donna, 1966–
    The Christmas promise / Donna VanLiere. —1st ed.
        p. cm.
    ISBN-13: 978-0-312-36776-3
    ISBN-10: 0-312-36776-7
    1. Interpersonal relations—Fiction.   2. Christmas stories.
I. Title.

    PS3622.A66C479   2007
    813'.6—dc22   2007020320

First Edition: October 2007

10   9   8   7   6   5   4   3   2   1

For David,
whose heart beats with the Promise

ACKNOWLEDGMENTS

Much appreciation to:

Troy, Gracie, and Kate, who fill my days with grace.

I always tell promising young writers that it's important to surround yourself with a great team. I have a brilliant group around me. They include my agents, Jennifer Gates and Esmond Harmsworth, my editor, Jennifer Enderlin, and many people at St. Martin's Press, including Matt Baldacci, John Karle, Carrie Hamilton-Jones, Lisa Senz, Matthew Shear, Nancy Trypuc, Mike Storrings for the beautiful cover, the entire sales staff who pound the pavement, and Sally Richardson for leading the way.

The AA members of Franklin, who were gracious enough to let me sit in on their meetings.

Nate Larkin, Rusty Owens, Mike O'Neill, and his son Michael O'Neill, who provided invaluable insight.

The Orchard Church in Franklin. Special thanks to Chris Carter for reading an early version of the manuscript and giving me feedback.

Sarah and Carrie Drumheller for being such crafty geniuses.

"Miss" Pam Dillon, "Miss" Jamie Betts, and "Mrs." Laurie Griffith at Little School for your heart.

Lindsey Wolford, whose help was priceless this past year. Just so we're clear, *you're* telling the girls that you're moving to Ireland, not me!

And to Bailey, who stayed by my side as long as he could.

The
Christmas
Promise

What do we live for, if not to make the world
a less difficult place for each other.
—George Eliot

Present Day

A fresh blanket of snow fell last night. Sparkling white mounds sit on top of the shrubs outside my kitchen window. I fall into a chair at the table and pour cream into my coffee. My friend Jack is working on a car in my driveway; I can see his breath in the air. I haven't known Jack long, only a year. "The Year of Wonders," I call it. I'm still trying to piece the year together but I don't think I ever will. Maybe I'm not supposed to; that's the beauty of the mystery.

When I was a young mother I loved to see the Christmas season begin. The day after Thanksgiving I'd put in my favorite cassette of songs with Bing Crosby, Rosemary Clooney, and Burl Ives, and the sounds of Christmas would fill our home as I hauled down the wooden Nativity set from the attic along with a battered fake tree. My children and husband and I would decorate it, and by the time we were finished it was always icicle heavy and bulb poor, but we took pictures as if the tree were standing on the White House lawn.

One winter, my youngest son, Matthew, pressed his nose to the living room window and watched the snow fall, covering our lawn. "Now it's Christmas," he had said.

"Snow doesn't make Christmas," I had said. "There are a lot of states and countries that never see a flake of snow. It's the promise of Christmas that makes Christmas what it is."

Matthew watched the snow cover the grass. "Promise of what?"

I sat on the floor next to him. "Well, it's the promise of love and grace. Grace was given to us at Christmas. That's the biggest promise of all."

My husband, Walt, thought it would be an adventure if the family trekked out to cut down our own tree that year. We bundled up the kids and drove to a friend's farm where Walt led us through what felt like miles of pastureland before we arrived at a small thicket of woods. My son Daniel spotted the perfect tree and Walt whacked at the bottom branches so he could get a clear shot at the trunk. Walt hadn't thought about sharpening the ax before we left that morning, and after several whacks he was tired and leaning up against a tree to catch his breath. Each of our children attempted to carve away at the tree, but of course they were all too small to do much damage. Walt was angry with himself for not sharpening the ax. Though I tried to stifle my laughs, I couldn't. He got down on his belly and was whittling away at the trunk as if with a pocketknife, and I laughed harder as the pine needles poked and jabbed at his face. He kicked at the trunk several times, bouncing off the branches and landing on the ground. The kids began to squeal as they watched him and soon they were running around the tree, giggling and kicking at it. Walt whacked, whittled, and lashed out at that tree until it finally surrendered and we laughed all the way back over the pastureland to the car.

For seven years of my life I dreaded to see Christmas come. I had lost my husband and youngest son within two weeks of each other, and those sweet memories with my family proved to be too painful to remember but devastating to forget.

It's a terrifying thing to give your heart to that small band of people around you, knowing that relationships can be messy and that someday your heart may be broken and you'll come undone. That's the riskiest part of this human journey. In the past year, I think I've finally learned that there are some things that God doesn't want us to forget so He allows us to go back to those memories—not daily, but on occasion—and remember. It's in those moments we discover that somehow, some way, God entwines both remembering and forgetting and shapes them into beauty, something that actually makes sense of the mess in our lives. I still have a hard time understanding that kind of grace, and although there are days when I feel unworthy to accept it, I do. If I didn't, I'd go crazy. We all would.

This story is about a lot of people; I've just been designated to tell it. There are days when I look back on the last year and think, *How did it all come together?* Then there are days when I wonder why it all couldn't have happened sooner. But it's every day that I know that in spite of us grace will prevail. That's the promise of Christmas.

November, one year earlier

I still think that the greatest suffering is being lonely,
feeling unloved, just having no one. . . . That is the worst
disease that any human being can ever experience.
—Mother Teresa

I peeked through the kitchen drapes that morning
and rushed to grab a bucket and rag. *Looks like a nice
one,* I said to myself, straining to see out the window.
Someone had left a refrigerator in my driveway. I
squeezed dishwashing liquid into the bottom of the
bucket and filled it with warm water, splashing my
hand till it disappeared in suds. I tied up my running
shoes—the sassy pink neon ones with the green
stripes—and slipped a bottle of household cleaner
into my coat pocket. A blown porch light stopped me
on the steps and I looked up at it. "Good grief. That
bulb didn't last very long. I need to get one of those
bulbs that last a year." I stepped into the kitchen and
reached to the top shelf of the utility closet. Back on

the porch, I unscrewed the old bulb from the bottom of the light casing. "There you go," I said, screwing in the new one.

I turned to the refrigerator in the driveway, sizing it up. "Not too big. Twenty cubic feet, I'd guess." I opened the door and backed away, holding my hand over my nose. "I'll have you cleaned and find a new home for you by lunchtime," I said, slipping on a pair of bright yellow latex gloves. I was used to talking to myself; I'd been a widow for seven years. I was never concerned about talking to myself; what worried me is how I answered myself, and I was *really* troubled when I argued with myself! I pulled out one shelf after another, soaking my rag and scrubbing at unrecognizable globs of petrified food. I sprayed down the inside and tackled the back wall with a vengeance.

"There *is* a junk law, you know!" I cringed at hearing that familiar voice and closed my eyes. Maybe if I couldn't see her she wouldn't actually be there. "The city has mandated codes." I scrubbed harder. "Gloria Bailey, I'm talking to you."

How I despised that tone. I took a breath and lifted my head to see my neighbor standing on the other side of her fence. "Good morning, Miriam."

"Gloria, does anyone ever bother to let you know that they're dropping this rubbish off?"

I shoved my head inside the fridge, scrubbing at the walls. I once told my friend Heddy that there wasn't enough room in the cosmos for Miriam's ego. Her affected British accent was as real as her blond hair and her name. Miriam Lloyd Davies. Come on! "It'll be gone by noon, Miriam," I said, wringing out the rag.

"I doubt it, by the looks of it," Miriam said. "But if it's not gone I'll need to have it hauled out of here. I don't pay taxes to live next to a junkyard."

It's amazing how perfect your posture becomes when you've been insulted. Every vertebra in my back straightened to supreme alignment as I walked up the driveway. "I don't pay taxes to live next to a junkyard!" I said, whispering.

When I moved into my home six years ago a lovely young couple with two small children lived in the house next door. They were always polite, smiling and waving each day, even leaving a present on my doorstep each Christmas. If my work annoyed them, they never showed it. Miriam moved in three years ago when the young couple found themselves expecting a third child and in need of a larger home. She was graceful and statuesque—fitting for a stage actress and professor's wife—but I found her to be cold and distant, although her husband, Lynn, was always gracious and warm. Lynn died a year after moving into the home. I tried on several occasions to befriend Miriam, assuming our widow status would assure some sort of bond between us, but just because someone is plopped into your life doesn't mean a friendship will be forged.

I often felt pasted together, compared to Miriam's refined look. I looked my age (sixty and proud of it) while Miriam denied hers (fifty and holding). I've never been what you could call fashionable, but I take pride in my appearance. I like my clothes to match and am most comfortable in cotton and jersey (but no belts). I don't wear anything that hurts! Miriam preferred slacks with a designer blouse or cashmere sweater and she was always neat, nothing disheveled about her. Her hair was the color of golden honey and framed her face in a chic bob. She promptly made her next appointment at the beauty salon for five weeks to the date of her last cut and coloring. My hair was salt and pepper (more salt than pepper) and hung in soft, or rather, annoying curls around my face. When it got too long I simply bobby-pinned it back until I found the time to give myself a trim.

I walked into the kitchen and dialed a number on the phone, listening as it rang in my ear. I was about to hang up when the line clicked on the other end. "Hello! Heddy?" I said. "I've got a fridge. Can you look through the list and see who needs what?"

I heard Heddy rustling through papers. Dalton Gregory was the retired school superintendent and his wife, Heddy, was a nurse at the hospital who was on duty when I had my gallbladder taken out four years ago. *We've been taking stuff from you ever since,* Heddy once said. I couldn't do my work without them. They had the organizational skills that I sorely lacked. I relied on sticky notes and miscellaneous paper scraps to remind myself of appointments or calls, and my idea of filing was stacking things on the kitchen table. Dalton and Heddy kept everything on computer and could pull it up with the touch of a finger. I still wasn't entirely sure how to turn on a computer.

"A family with three children called yesterday," Heddy said. "Their refrigerator broke four days ago and the father is in the hospital. The mother hasn't had any time to look for a new one."

I peered through the drapes and watched Miriam nosing around the refrigerator. I shook my head, watching her. "Can Dalton come pick it up and deliver it?" I rapped on the window and Miriam jumped, making me laugh. She threw her nose in the air and marched to her own yard. "Sooner than later, Heddy. Miriam Lloyd Snooty Face is riding her broom again."

Years earlier, I had been driving home late one winter night when, near the downtown bridge, I noticed a homeless man with a red hat who wasn't wearing socks with his shoes. I couldn't get the image of the man out of my mind. What if that had been my own son? Would anyone have helped? Days later I walked into Wilson's Department Store and found socks for ninety-nine cents a pair in a discount bin at the back of the store. "What would it cost if I bought the whole bin?" I had asked owner Marshall Wilson.

"Tell you what," Marshall had said. "I'll donate all these *and* hats and scarves to your cause." I hadn't realized I was championing a "cause," but when I delivered the clothes out of the back of my trunk I knew that the cause had found me. People needed help right in my own backyard. I had been slumping around and feeling sorry for myself long enough and needed to do something about it.

"Thank you, Miss Glory," the man with the red hat had said. The name Miss Glory stuck. Since that time I'd taken in whatever I could get my hands on and given it out to the homeless and families in need, especially young single mothers with children. My husband and I had four children and I couldn't imagine having raised them by myself.

I taught cooking in my home along with simple classes like how to make a budget and basic child care. Dalton taught computer and job interviewing courses, but all our classes were small. I didn't have the space in my house for large groups.

"He'll be there in a bit," Heddy said. "Then Miriam won't have anything to complain about."

"I doubt that," I said.

"Gloria?" Heddy's voice changed and I wondered what was wrong. "We got word that Rikki Huffman was charged with drug possession last night."

I fell into a chair at the kitchen table. Rikki was a single mom I'd been working with for the last two years who seemed to be getting her feet on the ground. "No! She was doing so great. Where is she?"

"They have her at County." Heddy was quiet.

"She'll spend time in jail with this offense, Gloria." I assumed that, but still hoped Heddy would say something else. "Are you all right?"

"Not really," I said, rubbing my head. "Who has her kids?"

"DFS. The Department of Family Services will place them. Maybe they already have. You've done everything you could for Rikki. You know that, right?"

I sighed. "My mind knows that, sure."

"Rikki just can't break the cycle," Heddy said. I was quiet. "Gloria? Gloria!"

I jumped at her voice. "Yes."

"Don't blame yourself." That always proved to be easier said than done for me. "You can't save everyone. It's not your job."

I hung up the phone and sat at the table, thinking about Rikki for the longest time. I nursed a cup of coffee before heading back outside.

"I'm going on holiday for five days, Gloria."

I turned to see Miriam behind the fence. That sounded wonderful to me. After learning about Rikki's arrest I wasn't in the mood to have Miriam breathing down my neck at every turn. "That's great," I said. "It's always good for you to go away." That didn't come out right. "I mean, good for you to leave." I was making it worse, and put on the most sincere fake smile I could muster.

"It's my birthday," she said. "My daughter and her family have asked me to celebrate with them. One only turns fifty once, you know!"

A loud gust of air shot over my teeth before I could rein it back in. "Ha!" Miriam's eyes narrowed, looking at me. "Fifty! Well . . . congratulations . . . *again*," I added, under my breath.

"Would you watch the house for me?"

"Of course," I said.

"Just keep an eye open and notify the police if anyone drops off any unsightly rubbish."

I cringed. It was really hard to like that woman.

The bus was packed that morning. Several people had shoved their backpacks up against the window to eke out a few minutes of sleep between stops. Twenty-four-year-old Chaz McConnell sat next to a fat man who was somehow under the impression that he had rights to Chaz's seat as well. Chaz spent the majority of the ride claiming his armrest and foot space while watching the snow fall outside.

The bus drove through the town square and

pulled in front of the bus stop, which was nothing more than a small storefront a few blocks from town with a bench in front of it. Chaz grabbed his backpack and inched his way out of the seat; the fat man never bothered to get up. Chaz pulled the hood of his sweatshirt up and saw apartments just up the street. A one-bedroom apartment was available and he could move in after he paid a one-month deposit and the first month's rent. He pulled out a wad of money and walked into the apartment with everything he owned stuffed into a backpack. Later in the day he saw a futon and its frame by the Dumpster and made his way across the parking lot to check it out. He noticed that the owner of the house across the road was replacing Christmas lights on the trees in front of his home.

"Those lights have been up all year," a neighbor woman said when she saw Chaz looking at them. "They keep them on all the time." The neighbor woman kept talking about the lights but Chaz ignored her, examining the futon frame. One leg was broken but he knew he could just prop it up on something and have a suitable bed. He dragged it up the three flights of stairs to his apartment and put it against the pale beige wall in the bedroom. Days later he found a small black-and-white TV with poor reception by the Dumpster, and a few days after that a card table. He used milk crates as chairs for the table and drawers for the few clothes he owned. As far as he was concerned, he had all the furniture he needed.

When Chaz started the walk to Wilson's Department Store on Monday it was barely drizzling, but when he approached the town square there was a deluge. The streetlamps had been wrapped with evergreen and topped off with red bows. Several of the storefronts were decorated for the Christmas season, including the barbershop, which had managed to put a waving Santa in the front window to announce the special cut and shave of the week. When he passed the church on the square, several people were coming out of the basement and darting for their cars. He meandered between them and pulled the hood of his sweatshirt over his head, making a dash for the entrance of Wilson's. It was busy inside, but that was to be expected right before Thanksgiving. He took off his sweatshirt and held it away from himself, running his fingers through soggy hair.

"Good morning," a sales associate said behind a

stack of ladies' sweaters she was carrying. "Can I help you find anything?"

"Mr. Wilson told me to come in this morning to fill out paperwork for a job."

"The office is just up the stairs behind the purses." The stack of sweaters tumbled to the floor but Chaz ignored them, walking past the salesgirl toward the small flight of stairs. The store was old: As he looked at the elevators, his guess was it dated back to the early 1950s, but they'd done a lot of remodeling over the years. The floor on the main aisle was made of bright white tiles. The cosmetics and jewelry counters faced each other on the main aisle, and oversized lit Christmas stars and bulbs dangled from the ceiling above each counter. The men's and women's departments were on either side of the main aisle, with carpeting in shades of burgundy and green. Beyond the cosmetics counter were shoes and ladies' handbags, and the stairs leading to the office.

Chaz took the stairs by two and found the small office. A woman wearing a red sweater covered with green and silver beaded ornaments was on the phone. She had a small sign on her desk that read JUDY LUITWEILER. "I'm sorry," she said when she hung up the receiver. "My daughter's having a baby any day now

and I keep calling her. Anxious grandma, you know!"
She spun her hands in the air and Chaz tried to smile
but was too wet to care.

"I'm supposed to start work today. They told me to
come up here for the paperwork."

"Sure. Sure," Judy said, opening a metal file drawer
behind her desk. "What's your name?"

"Chaz McConnell."

She rifled through the files like a squirrel after a
nut. "And which department will you be in?"

"Security."

"Sure. Sure," she said, pulling a manila folder from
the cabinet. "Do you have any children?" she asked,
sorting the papers. "We love children around here."

"No, I don't."

"Morning, Chaz." Marshall Wilson stepped down
from the office behind Judy's, wearing jeans and a
denim shirt. "How are you, son?" No one had called
Chaz son in years and the word sounded odd to him.

"Fine. How are you?"

"Better than I deserve to be at my age, I'm certain
of that," Marshall said. "Did you get settled into a
place?" Chaz nodded. "We're ramping up for a busy
Christmas season, so we're glad you're here."

"You must be Chaz." Chaz turned to see a black

man dressed in dark pants and a gray shirt with a badge attached to the left side of his chest pushing his way into the cramped office. The man stretched out his hand and Chaz wiped his off on his jeans before shaking. "I'm Ray Burroughs. I'll be training you." Chaz summed him up: He was about his size, maybe a little heavier, but he knew he was going to look as dorky as Ray did in that uniform. "Come on down to the office. You can fill out the papers there and get something dry to put on."

Chaz followed as Ray ran down two flights of stairs to the break room. He pointed to the time clock on the wall. "Clock in here when your shift starts." He took the card with Chaz's name on it and handed it to him so he could punch in, then led him down the hall. He glanced down at Chaz's soggy shoes. "Did you walk here?"

"Yeah."

"Don't you have a car?"

"I did. It was stolen a couple of months ago." The truth was, Chaz had owed some small gambling debts to a guy a few towns ago and the man had taken the car as payment. Chaz didn't care; he thought it was a piece of junk anyway.

"Are you going to walk to work every day?" Ray asked.

"Yeah."

"Then you'd better invest in an umbrella." The top of the office door was etched glass. The word SECURITY was written in black block letters in the middle of the window. They stepped inside. The walls were brick, but someone had painted them off-white. Four video monitors sat on the large desk in the center of the room with images from select departments in the store. Ray pointed to a black vinyl sofa against the wall. "You can sit there if you want, or here at the desk. It doesn't matter." Chaz looked at the desk covered with papers, files, and cups of old coffee, and opted for the couch. Ray sat on the wooden swivel chair at the desk and leaned back. The thick spring whined beneath him. "So, word is that Mr. Wilson hired you away from another store?"

"That's right," Chaz said, filling out the first line.

"How long did you work security there?"

"I didn't," Chaz said. "I stocked shelves."

"Then how'd you get hired for security?"

. . .

Chaz had been living in a town an hour away when he met Marshall Wilson. For the first time in his life he was working in a retail store rather than in a restaurant as a waiter or cook. Chaz was stacking men's jeans in cubbies that stretched to the ceiling when Marshall needed assistance, but Chaz wasn't paying attention—his eye was on a young woman pushing a baby stroller. The baby was asleep and the woman was discreet as she first put a pair of pants and then a sweater into the bottom of the stroller, covering the items with the baby's blanket and diaper bag. "You forgot a belt to go with that outfit," Chaz whispered as he moved past her toward his cart filled with denim. Her back stiffened as she flung the goods onto the clothing table in front of her and fled the store. The baby never wakened. Chaz laughed as he watched her and climbed back onto the ladder to replenish the top row of jeans.

"You handled that well," Marshall said.

"Thanks," Chaz said without looking down.

"Would you be interested in changing jobs?"

Chaz stacked four pair of jeans into the top cubby. "Nope."

"I need another security guard at the store. I'm sure it pays better than what you make here."

Chaz looked down and saw an elderly man with white hair wearing jeans and a red plaid flannel shirt. *Probably owns a hardware store*, Chaz thought. "I'm listening," he said, shoving the pair of jeans he had wedged under his arm on top of the stack.

A full-time job sounded good to Chaz at that point. *There's a great cure for being broke*, his mother used to say. *Go to work*. He didn't like to stay in one place too long and was ready for a change. Chaz was always ready for a change. With every move he'd think, *Okay, this time I'll do better. I'll be better. I'll change.* But he never did. He couldn't. But this time he really thought he could make it stick, so he packed his bags.

"What kind of guy is Mr. Wilson?" Chaz asked.

Ray took a sip of coffee from one of the cups on the desk and grimaced: obviously not the one he was looking for. "He may not look the part of a department store owner, but he knows what he's doing. Not a lot of gray area with him. He's to the point. He won't stand over you and watch you work. The way I see it, he figures you got a job to do, so do it. If you don't do it, then there are other people who will."

"So he stays out of your business?"

Ray swallowed something out of another cup and shook his head in disgust. "Unless you're doing something that makes him *get* up in your business." He put his feet on the floor and leaned toward him. "You married?"

"No," Chaz said.

"Got a girlfriend?"

"No."

"Why not?" Chaz stopped and looked up at him. Ray raised his hands. "Just asking. You're a good-looking guy. Keep yourself in shape. No love handles. Just seems like you'd be married or have a girlfriend."

"I do okay," Chaz said, writing his Social Security number.

"I did okay, too, until I got married. Now I do what she says." Ray broke out laughing and leaned forward, shoving a picture in Chaz's face. "These are my kids: Alexandra's four and Joseph is two."

"Cute," Chaz said, glancing up.

"Cute nothing. They're downright gorgeous. Look again."

"Yeah. Really cute."

Ray shook his head and put the picture back among the mess on the desk. "Man, you don't know anything about etiquette." Chaz looked up at him.

"You're supposed to flatter somebody when you talk about their kids. Be sure to remember that when Mrs. Grobinski comes into the store with her ugly twins." He pounded the desk, laughing at himself. He watched as Chaz filled in the blank lines on the form. "I only work thirty hours a week because I go to school for computer programming. You in school?"

"No," Chaz said. Ray leaned forward and Chaz knew there would be a fresh onslaught of questions. "What do you do all day as a security guard?" he asked, distracting Ray.

Ray leaned back in the chair and folded his hands on top of his chest. "The biggest part of this job is being a courtesy officer," he said. Mr. Marshall told Chaz he needed a security guard, not a courtesy officer. What sort of wimp job was that? It sounded like it should come with an atomizer and a napkin folded over his arm. "You want to walk through the departments and make sure the employees are all right, ask them if anything's wrong that you need to know about. Every now and then they'll signal to you to keep your eye on somebody who might look fishy. It's your job to walk through the department so that person sees you and the badge and uniform."

"But you don't carry a gun?"

"We're not cops," Ray said. "We can't arrest anybody. Remember that if you see somebody stealing something and you call them on it. If they pull a knife or gun, just back up and say, 'Let me get the door for you.' Our job is to prevent theft, not get in fisticuffs with thieves."

Chaz watched as Ray pointed out the video monitors. "One of us is usually back here on the monitors and that person will radio the guy on the floor and tell him about suspicious behavior."

"What if you catch somebody?" Chaz said.

"You write them up and leave it up to management if they want to call the police and press charges. A huge part of the job, especially now at Christmas, is to carry customers' bags to their cars." Chaz looked up at Ray. "I know. You had envisioned guns and glory and you get bags of towels instead." Chaz went back to the paperwork. "We also help parents find their lost toddlers, help the elderly in and out of their cars, help people find their keys they lost somewhere in the store, and we fix a *lot* of flat tires."

"Is that it?"

"We make sure that nobody hurts Santa or destroys his workshop."

Chaz stopped writing. "We're security guards for Santa?"

Ray smiled and nodded. "He shows up every morning from nine till noon and each evening from five till eight. Some kids will beat the crap out of the big lollipops and candy canes, and a few of them get pretty rough with the big man." Ray took a breath. "And! We answer a lot of questions like, 'What do you think of this dress?' 'If you were my husband would you like these pants?' or 'Do you think these shoes are cute?' But no matter *what* you think, always be courteous. Our job is to treat the customer with respect and be as helpful as we can. This time of year we rack up lots of overtime and can make some decent money." The money part caught Chaz's attention. He knew that if he could just make enough to move on to something better, he'd be happy. "Think you can handle it?"

"Sure," Chaz said, with as much enthusiasm as he could rally.

Ray pulled open a drawer and ripped into a small bag of chips. "Are you from here?"

Chaz shook his head.

"Where're you from?"

"I've moved around a lot."

"Army brat?"

"No."

"Where were you originally from?" Ray asked. "Where do your parents live?"

"My parents are dead."

"I'm sorry, man. You got brothers or sisters?"

"No."

"No wonder you move around a lot." Ray handed Chaz a uniform. "Maybe you'll find something to keep you here for a while."

Chaz forced a smile but knew he wouldn't stay here, either.

Early that evening Chaz unloaded a bag of groceries onto the kitchen counter and pulled out a case of beer, opening one can. He'd taken his first drink when he was fourteen at a neighbor's house down the street. He drank what he could get away with in high school but that wasn't much; his mother had been a watch-dog. She told him he was bent for self-destruction but he ignored her; he got to the point where he ignored everything she said. Once he was out of the house it was easier to party and he eventually found himself thinking about when, where, and how he'd get his next drink. He once worked with a guy who told him he drank too much and Chaz had told him to go to hell. He drank cheap beer, no hard liquor, and a few beers made him feel ten feet tall inside and helped him forget what he'd done. Something had to make him feel good about what he'd become. He looked at the stark walls and sank into the cushions on the futon. His father once said that we all have wild horses deep inside us. As a child, Chaz was unsure of what he meant, but over the years those horses had driven him to do things he never imagined.

When he was a boy in third grade Chaz sat with his class and watched a film about researchers sifting through the debris of Mount Saint Helens. When the volcano erupted in 1980, the lava actually melted away the soil. Naturalists wondered how long it would take before anything would ever grow there again. Then one day a park employee stumbled across a patch of grass, ferns, and wildflowers in the shape of an elk. "They were growing right out of a dead animal," Chaz had told his parents. "Isn't that gross?"

"I think it's amazing," his father had said. "Shows that life always makes a way." Chaz held firm that what happened on Mount Saint Helens was eerie and disgusting, but his parents rarely ever saw the repulsive side of something: It seemed they were always looking for signs of life, and that annoyed him to no end.

Days later, Chaz found himself still talking about the flowers. "God's in the smallest detail," his mother had said as he helped her decorate the tree. "We see something as the end but He sees it as the beginning."

"Beginning of what?" Chaz had asked.

"New life," his mother had said, stretching to hang a bulb at the top of the tree. "God's in that market, you know, but a lot of times we forget that."

"Why do we forget?"

She wrapped a strand of gold garland around the top of the tree. "Oh, I don't know. Blurry vision, I guess. It's easy to lose our vision when we get bogged down in everyday stuff. We just get in a rush and without really knowing it we leave God behind."

"Then why doesn't He get closer?"

"We're the ones who move," she had said. "God never moves." She leaned over and bent her head close to his ear. "Don't forget that."

"I won't forget," he had said.

But he did. Chaz pushed aside the memories and

meaning of Christmas until there wasn't anything left but him and he found himself dreading the season that his parents had loved. "It's just a bunch of people pretending," he would say. Who knows when he made the leap from innocence to disbelief, but it had happened.

Perhaps if his parents had been with him he wouldn't have lost his way, but without them he had no compass. He convinced himself that peace on earth and joy to the world existed only in sappy songs, not in the real world. In the real world there was rape and murder, disease, and child hunger. Not even Christmas, with its promises of goodwill to all, could fix its multitude of problems.

He took a long drink. Outside the door he heard a couple with a small child maneuvering a Christmas tree through the breezeway. "Wait, wait, wait," the woman shouted. "I can't go that fast!"

The man bellowed a laugh and the child giggled. "What are you doing back there?" the man said.

"I swear something just fell out of the tree and crawled on me," the woman shrieked. More laughter from the happy family. Chaz turned on the TV to drown them out. Why had he come to this town? Now it seemed like a stupid idea. He was better off working job to job instead of committing to something long-term, especially this close to Christmas, which was a day he endured at best. The couple shoved the tree through their front door to more peals of laughter. He opened another beer and stared at the TV screen. This town was no better than the last, and nothing could make him stay. Unlike his parents, he could never see the rays of hope or sprigs of life clinging to devastation. At least that's what he thought.

TWO

From what we get, we can make a living;
what we give, however, makes a life.
—Arthur Ashe

I ran down the stairs pulling a red sweatshirt with a
Christmas tree on it over my head. "Hold on! I'm
coming!" The phone rang again. I always tried to answer by the third ring before it went to voice mail.
"Get out of the way, Whiskers." The cat jumped from
his spot on the bottom step and ran in front of me to
the kitchen.

"Miss Glory, they shut off my electricity." It was
Carla Sanchez.

"Why'd they do that?" I asked, catching my
breath.

"I was late paying. . . ."

"How late?"

"Just a few days," Carla said.

"They don't shut off your electricity if you're just a few days late. How late?"

"Almost three months. But I got a job now. I'm down at Wilson's just like you said. They still had the sign in the window when I went down and they hired me just like that."

"How's Donovan?" I asked.

"He's good."

"What'd he eat for breakfast?" There was silence on the other end. "What's he going to eat for lunch?" More silence followed. "Let me see what I can do." I hung up the phone before dialing the number for the church I attended. "Linda, it's Gloria. Can I talk with Rod?" I joined the church six years ago, shortly after moving to town to be closer to my oldest daughter, who'd had a baby. The church was always the first to help when I needed something for my work, but I was careful not to take advantage of their good graces. I listened to Christmas music until Rod picked up his line. "How are you, Rod?"

"Great," he said. "What's happening, Gloria?"

Rod was always willing to listen. "I have a single mom who needs help," I said. I explained Carla's circumstances and waited.

"How much is the bill?" Rod asked.

He said he'd have a check made out to the electric company waiting at the church and told me about a car that had been donated to the church. "It came in a few days ago," he said. "The title work is taken care of and someone is bringing it to you today or tomorrow." I had been in Rod's office years earlier when a car had been donated to the church. A family with whom I worked was in dire need, and the church and I struck up a working relationship.

Something caught my eye in the driveway and I pushed back the curtain, clapping. "It's already here," I said. "Thanks so much, Rod. Talk to you soon." I hung up the phone and pressed close to the window. "Well look at that! She's a beauty." I bolted for the door and pulled on a pair of knee-length yellow rubber boots with tops that folded down to reveal blue wool inside. One pant leg stayed hoisted above the boot but I didn't care. "That's a Chevy, isn't it? Silver. I'll call her the Silver Fox." I swung open the driver's side door and slid inside, turning the key. The engine grinded and I waited. I turned the key again and the engine wheezed before choking quiet. "I'll get somebody out here to take a look at you ASAP," I said, patting the steering wheel.

I hustled back up the porch stairs and picked up

the phone in the kitchen, dialing the number for my mechanic. "Jerry? It's Gloria. Somebody left a Chevy that looks about eight or so years old. Would you have any time to look at it?" I looked out the window and examined the car.

"Midge and I are headed out of town today," Jerry said. "Her father had a stroke and is in the hospital. I don't know when we'll be back, but I can look at it then."

"I'm so sorry, Jerry. Don't even think about it."

I hung up and pulled out the yellow pages, turning to "car repair," but then I threw the book on the table. "I can't think about that now." There just weren't enough hours in the day. I flew to the garage.

Every wall was lined with shelves that held food items, pots and pans, dishware, towels, and supplies such as toilet tissue and paper towels. In the middle of the floor were racks of clothing sorted by size. I rummaged through the shelves and loaded peanut butter, crackers, soup, rice, and cereal into a box.

The electric garage door had long been blocked with shelves, so I lugged the box back into the kitchen. I slipped on my coat, the soft jean jacket one with huge patchwork pockets on the front, then pulled a yellow wool hat down over my ears. Heddy said the boots and the hat together made me look like Big Bird, but I was warm so I didn't care.

I wanted to add milk, eggs, and bread to the box of food for Carla, so I made a stop at the local grocery. My daughter Stephanie called me while I was in the store; she usually checked in with me two to three times a week. "How's your week?" she asked.

"Great, except Rikki Huffman is in jail for drug possession," I said.

She sighed on the other end. "I'm sorry, Mom. You did all you could."

I grabbed a gallon of milk off the shelf. "That's what Heddy said." I reached for a dozen eggs and put them in my basket.

"What are you doing today?" Stephanie asked.

"Just seeing to some things," I said.

"Seeing Matt in every face?" she said, referring to my youngest son.

I tossed bread into my basket and headed for the checkout. "Of course not. I'm not crazy, Stephanie." I knew my children worried about me. My remaining two sons had long kept quiet about Matthew, but Stephanie wore her heart on her sleeve.

"I know you're not, Mom, but . . ." She was quiet. "It's been years since—"

"I know," I said, stopping her. It was a daily sorrow of which I didn't need to be reminded. I felt my throat tighten. "Kiss the boys for me and we'll talk soon." I threw the phone in my purse, grabbed my sack of groceries, and left the store.

I drove to Carla's apartment. Donovan, a five-year-old ball of fire, greeted me at the door. I pretended to fall over. "You scared me to death!" I said. He laughed, watching me clutch my heart. "Are my eyes bugged out of my head? It feels like my eyes are bugged out of my head."

Donovan lifted my eyelids and shook his head. "Nope. They're in your head."

"What color are my eyes, Donovan?"

He looked at me hard. "Red!"

I bent over laughing, lifting the box of Cheerios out of the sack. Donovan tore into the top and I pushed him toward the kitchen. "Don't eat out of the box. You're not a bear."

Carla pulled her straight, black hair into a ponytail and I sat down, looking at her. Donovan obviously got his curly hair from his father, whoever he was.

"Has Thomas been living here again?" I never tip-toed around what was on my mind. Some people would say I lacked tact, but after years of knowing her I had learned how to communicate with Carla.

"No, Miss Glory."

"Because if he has been and he's been sucking you dry for money and food and a place to live, then—"

"He doesn't know where I live now. I promise."

"Do you want to see him?" I asked. Carla turned her head away. She looked much older than her age, but she'd lived a lot of life in twenty-three years. "Carla, God didn't create you for this. He didn't create anybody for this." She wouldn't look at me. "That man uses you. He hurts you." Carla wasn't listening. She'd heard it all before from so many others.

A string of losers. That's what Carla's mother called her boyfriends when I talked to her on the phone. *The next one worse than the last.* When Carla had been pregnant with Donovan, she had hoped his father would stay, but he didn't. No man ever stayed. Thomas had been with her longer than the others, and Carla thought they could be a family, but she was wrong.

I sighed. "Is your wrist better?"

Carla rolled her wrist to show the movement she

had again. "It's much better. I didn't even have to take all the pain pills the doctor prescribed."

I kept my voice low. "One day he could come in here and hurt you right in front of Dovovan. He may even hurt Donovan."

"I'm not going to see him anymore, Miss Glory."

"If he comes back, call the police and they'll get rid of him," I said.

"I can't do that, Miss Glory," she said, whispering.

I sat forward. "Call the police before he hurts you again."

Tears fell down her cheeks. "If I call them they might come in and take Donavan away from me again." I shook my head. Her voice rose louder. "DFS will find out about the police and they'll take him."

I put my hands on her shoulders. "They won't take your son because you're trying to protect him. . . ." I reached for a tissue in my pocket and wiped her face. "If he comes back, promise me that you'll call the police."

"I will, Miss Glory."

I had heard that before, but wanted to believe her. I stood and took Carla's hand, leading her into the kitchen. I unpacked the food into the cupboards and opened the refrigerator. "Milk should always be in

your refrigerator. Donovan needs it and so do you."
She nodded; she knew that, but days would go by
without Donovan having a glass of milk or even a decent meal. I handed Carla the check. "Take this di-
rectly to the electric company. This is the last time I'll
be able to help pay it. You know that, don't you?"

She nodded. "I got that job, so I'll be able to pay all
my bills now."

I hugged her, saying how excited I was for her, and
bent over to kiss the top of Donovan's head. "*Adiós.*"

"Good-bye, Señorita Cuckoo." He giggled and
shoved a handful of Cheerios into his mouth.

I got into my car and waved. Carla waved back and
I prayed that this time she'd have the strength she
needed to keep Thomas out of her life.

A few days into the job Fred Clauson, the head of security, told Ray and Chaz that they'd have to rotate the
night shift till after Christmas. "It's supposed to be a
season of peace," Fred said. "But somebody manages
to break into the store around this time every year."
Chaz volunteered to take the shift by himself.

"We always rotate the night shift through Christmas," Ray said.

"I can work it," Chaz said, taking a swig of coffee. "It's no big deal." Actually, Chaz figured there were fewer people to deal with at night, so he could do what he wanted. He liked it that way.

"Why would you want to work solid nights for weeks on end?" Ray asked.

Chaz shrugged. "I don't know. It doesn't bother me."

"You are a hard one to crack," Ray said, slapping the top of the desk. He slid a stale chocolate-chip cookie from an open package in the bottom drawer into his mouth. "Just be sure you keep up with the job, you know. Being alone here at night isn't necessarily a good thing. It's easy to get distracted and forget about the work."

Chaz nodded. "Don't worry about it."

Ray leaned back in the chair and folded his hands on top of his head. "Uh-huh. You're thinking that Ray don't know jack, but in reality Ray's got your back!"

"The Robert Frost of the security team."

Ray laughed and flung himself forward in the chair. "Oh!" he said, sliding a note in front of Chaz. "Be sure to go see Judy in the office before the end of the day."

.   .   .

Chaz thought about going to the local sports bar at the end of the street throughout his shift. Drinking was the high point of his life, and he looked forward to it to cap off each day. At the end of his shift he grabbed his coat and ran for the door but stopped, remembering that he needed to see Judy. He ran up the stairs to the main office and let Judy roll one finger after another into ink before pressing them down into tiny squares on a card. "What did employers do before fingerprinting?" she said, chattering on about her new granddaughter. "Guess it was easier for convicted felons to find a job!" She placed the fingerprints into a large envelope and sealed it. "That's all there is to it," she said. "Simple as that." He rubbed his purplish blue fingertips together and walked out of the store toward the bar.

He jumped awake at four A.M. The room was stiflingly hot and he couldn't breathe; the sheets were covered with sweat. He sat up on the edge of the bed. Where did Judy say she was sending those fingerprints? To what screening company? "Simple as that," she had said, sealing the envelope. What had he done? How could he have made such a stupid mistake? He looked at the clock again: four oh-one. Judy wouldn't be at the store again until Monday morning. There wasn't anything he could do about it over the weekend. He bent over the bathroom sink and splashed water on his face, trying to figure a way out of the mess he'd just made. His hands started to shake and he walked to the kitchen, where he cracked open a can of beer. He downed it, but a current surged through his body and he drank three more beers before the shaking stopped.

His mother used to say that the most crucial lessons we learn aren't the ones we learn once but the ones that keep coming back, bending us till we nearly break. *Those are the ones that take longer to learn*, she had said once. Again and again he would do something that screwed up his life. He raced full bore into one situation after another, and in each town in which he lived, he just seemed to gain more speed until he ended up wounded and bruised in a ditch of his own making. He caught a glimpse of himself in the mirror that hung in the eating area. No matter how much he wanted to stop, he did the same things over and over again and despised himself for it. He was at the point where he lived in a perpetual state of dark equilibrium where he just sort of existed. Up until the last few months his life had always worked; he got by. Now, for whatever reason, it wasn't working any-more. He slumped to the floor, clutching the beer in his hand, and rested his head against the wall. He stayed there till dawn.

THREE

If the world seems cold to you,
kindle fires to warm it.
—Lucy Larcom

Chaz shook to at eleven on Monday morning and reached for a Xanax, downing three glasses of water with it. The pills weren't prescribed but he always knew where to get them, and he needed them to get through the day. He'd learned years earlier from a drinking buddy that his body would need a pill to help it get up and moving after a night of partying. The guy was right; a pill or two a day pulled Chaz together and allowed him to keep up with any coworker.

Mallory, an apartment tenant, was in the parking lot as he left his building, and she waved. Chaz had met her on several occasions in the parking lot and he dreaded seeing her. His parents said the Mallorys of the world were mannequin people. His father used to say, *Mannequin people try to look human but that's as close as they get. Their goal is just to get through life. They aren't concerned about you; it's all about them. They plod off to work and then back home, and along the way they buy a house and a car and everything they need. They never back an organization or get involved with a cause because it's too much trouble. They just exist and that's it.* Chaz knew his parents would have been saddened to see how easy it was for him to wander about without ever really knowing or caring about anyone else. He kept walking as Mallory blathered on about her recent dental work, her job, and high cholesterol. He walked faster and waved good-bye, bringing the conversation to an abrupt end.

On his way to work he saw the same crowd of people he had run into on his first day in town flowing out of the church basement on the town square. He bumped into a man and stumbled, nearly falling. The other guy did fall, landing on his can, and somebody pulled him up. "You okay, Frank?"

"Sorry, there!" The fallen man was yelling after

Chaz, but he blew him off. He needed to get to the mailroom. Keeping this job was his ticket to somewhere else and he intended to keep it till he had enough money. He hurried down the main aisle for the stairs.

"Chaz?" He jumped at Mr. Wilson's voice.

"Could you go out front and see to a homeless man? He's harmless, but customers never want to come inside the store when . . ." He waved his hand in the air. "You know what I mean." Chaz wanted to say that he wasn't officially on the clock yet, but nodded and ran to the front of the store. The sooner he took care of the problem, the quicker he could talk to Judy about the fingerprints.

The man was standing with his hands in his pockets and a gray wool cap pulled down over his ears. He was wearing a Carhartt coat that was too big for him, brown khakis, and work boots. His face was thin and a short beard covered it. Chaz was surprised, because he was either his age or younger. "Hi," Chaz said, approaching him.

"What's up?" the man said, keeping his hands in his pockets.

"Are you waiting for someone?" Chaz asked.

"Nope."

Chaz needed to get inside and was annoyed with this guy. "Do you need anything?"

"Nope."

Pulling teeth would be easier than a conversation with him. Chaz put his hands under his arms to keep them warm and looked out over the square. Someone was busy decorating three large fir trees by the gazebo. "I'm Chaz."

"Mike." Chaz searched his mind for something else to say. "Why don't you just tell me that the brass inside is uncomfortable with me standing here?" Mike said.

"It's the customers. You know."

"They're afraid I'll attack them and make off with their Gucci bags," Mike said. Chaz shrugged. "Don't worry. I'll leave. Trying to find my way around town. I just got off the bus a few days ago."

Chaz smiled and pulled out some dollar bills from his pocket. It was worth it to get the guy off the sidewalk. "For coffee and a meal. I'm new here, too, but they say Grimshaw's up the street has the best food in town."

Mike took the money and shoved it in his pocket. "The old ladies can breathe a sigh of relief now," he said, walking away.

Chaz ran inside the store and reeled past customers, pushing his way through two swinging doors that entered a room whose cinder-block walls were painted a pale yellow. Large mail bins lined one wall with each department the mail was intended for typewritten below each bin. White countertops made their way around two of the walls and they were covered with boxes and small packages. Huge industrial lights hung from the ceiling and he heard the bulbs buzzing above him. Two women, one around his age and the other in her midthirties, turned to look at him. "Hi, I'm Chaz," he said. The young one looked at him and smiled and he knew he had her where he needed her. He stepped toward her and smiled, manipulating and maneuvering, his MO for any situation. "I work in security."

"What can we do you for?" the older one asked.

"I'm sorry. I didn't even ask you your name," Chaz said.

"Tricia."

"And I'm Kelly," the young one said, leaning back against the counter and pushing a strand of hair behind her ear.

"Are you the new guy?" Tricia asked. She was warming up to him.

"Does it show?"

"No. I heard they were replacing Ed after he retired. Finally retired! Are you married?"

"No," he said.

Tricia glanced to Kelly and smiled. "Where are you from?" Kelly said.

"All over, really."

"Do you have family nearby?" Tricia asked.

"No. My parents are deceased."

Tricia wrinkled her nose. "I always ask too many questions."

Chaz smiled and patted her on the back. "No, you didn't. You're great." He rubbed his hands together, thinking ahead. "Maybe you can help me out. Judy sent me down here to ask you to be on alert for a package that will be arriving from GKD Systems."

"What's that?" Tricia asked.

"It's a screening company and they're sending some materials here that must go through the security office first. You're in charge, right, Tricia?"

She shifted in her seat. "No. Bill's the manager down here, but he doesn't go through the mail when it comes in. We do."

"Do I need to ask him about this or is it something you two would be able to help with?" Chaz said.

"We can," Kelly said. "No problem. It'll be addressed to security, right?"

He smiled, pretending to be uncertain. "I don't think so. It will probably be addressed to Judy in the office, but security must screen it first before anyone opens it." They looked skeptical. "I guess GKD had some sort of nut job working for them who sent out hazardous materials wrapped in a common package. Of course, authorities dealt with that guy, but the whole thing makes Judy kind of nervous."

"Okay. Yeah. Right," Tricia said, writing the name of the company onto a sticky note and posting it in front of them. "We'll keep our eyes open and get it up to you guys."

"You can just get it to me, if you don't mind. I'd love to do something dangerous so I can tell all my friends." They laughed and Chaz faked a smile; he was weary of constantly figuring his way out of something. Perspiration stuck to his shirt as he pushed through the doors.

I pulled into a spot across the street from Wilson's and saw him from behind. He was wearing a university jacket with a blue hat and white tennis shoes, and carrying a backpack like my son's. I threw the car into park and walked after him. I rushed through the town square, hurrying past men and women who were bundled up for a day of shopping. He walked toward the gazebo and I reached for his arm. He turned in a snap and I felt blood rush to my face. "I'm sorry," I said, retreating. "I thought you were someone else." I was a fool. *What is wrong with you, Gloria? I thought. Running after people like a bull after a red cape.* I hurried toward Wilson's and my feet slid out beneath me, taking my breath away.

Robert Layton was the first to my side. "Morning, Glory!"

I blew the curls out of my face and searched the back of my head for the bobby pin. "That joke never gets old, does it, Robert?" He laughed, helping me up. "I wasn't made for winter." He held me steady as I straightened my coat, shoving the yellow hat back onto my head. One pant leg was riding above my boot and I pulled it down, stamping my foot to knock off the slushy mess on top of it.

"I saw you running after a man, Gloria. Has it really come to that?" I laughed. Robert picked up my gloves and handed them to me. "Besides your pride, is anything broken, cracked, or wounded?"

I brushed snow from my backside. "Well, my mother always told me that if I was going to fall to do so in front of a young man because he'd still be able to bend over and pick me up."

"I can't imagine that *anyone* in my office would call me young," Robert said, laughing. I had met Robert three years earlier at a charity function. He was an old friend of Dalton and Heddy's, and I found him to be pleasant and unassuming, quite the opposite of what I'd always imagined for a lawyer. "Is your work keeping you busy, Gloria?"

I clapped my hands together. "Just a few days ago I got a car. That doesn't happen very often, you know. That's very exciting for me and Heddy."

Robert pulled up the collar of his overcoat. "I bet it is."

I needed to get home, and I stepped into the street. "But I have to find a mechanic before my neighbor gets back into town."

Robert took me by the arm and opened the car door. "Call Jack Andrews at City Auto Service. He's done my work for years."

"I can't pay a lot," I said.

"He won't ask a lot. Gloria, you need a place where you can put all the stuff you collect."

"I got a place. My garage." I started the car and rolled down the window. "Thank you, Robert. Say hi to Kate."

He walked back to the sidewalk, shoving his hands in his coat pockets. "You bet. Let me know if I can ever do anything to help."

I scribbled Jack Andrews's name on a pad I kept in the car, and watched as a homeless man across the square pulled a hat farther down on his head. It was getting colder. I squinted to see who he was, wondering if he was new to town, but the light turned green before I could see his face, so I drove away.

My kitchen and living room were strewn with boxes filled with shampoo, soap, deodorant, toothpaste, and toothbrushes. Dalton and Heddy were helping me inventory what we had so we could figure out what items were still needed for care packages we'd be giving to the families with whom we worked and to the street people downtown. It was our fourth year putting the packages together, and each year we managed to add more things. I heard a car and looked up from the kitchen table to see Miriam pulling into her driveway.

"Do you hear that?" Heddy said. "Dogs have stopped barking. Birds have stopped chirping."

"She has a way of doing that," I said, watching Miriam drive into her garage. She'd been gone five days, but it felt like one glorious year without her next door. I worked at breaking down a box, but stopped when I heard something. "What was that?"

"Probably Jack working on the Silver Fox," Dalton said.

Heddy and I looked out the window when the noise grew louder, and saw Miriam shouting on her cell phone, waving her arms. I pressed closer to the window. "What is she doing?" Miriam's voice grew strident and shrill, and Heddy and I ran to the front door, leaving Dalton at the table.

"Everything! I mean everything," Miriam shouted. "How soon? I can't wait that long. I need someone over here now. Forget it!" She snapped the phone closed.

Jack Andrews was bent over the engine of the car, but lifted his head to listen. I shrugged my shoulders as I passed him, and walked into Miriam's yard. She looked as if she'd just stepped out of the pages of *Town & Country*, wearing her beautiful long camel-hair coat, black leather gloves, and fur-trimmed hat. "Miriam?"

She jumped. "What! What, Gloria?"

"Is something wrong?"

She pointed to her house. "Everything's destroyed. Everything." Her voice broke and Heddy and I walked up the front steps, opening the door. Water seeped over our shoes, startling us. "You're telling me you don't have one room? Not one single room?" Miriam was screaming. "I can't wait four days. I need a room now!"

My eyes widened as I watched water cascade down the living room wall. "I've never seen anything like this," Heddy said, whispering.

I reached to flick on the light switch but caught myself. "You didn't walk through there, did you?"

"I'm not an imbecile, Gloria," Miriam said.

Heddy leaned farther into the doorway and listened. "Is that a toilet running?"

I pointed upstairs. "It's probably been running since she's been gone," I whispered. "For five days." Heddy slapped her head.

"When will these *people* be leaving town?" Miriam was pacing up and down her driveway, shouting again. She hung up, defeated. "Every hotel is booked for the annual Christmas in the Colonies craft fair." She spat out the words. "Every room is filled with nutters dressed as Puritans!"

I knew what needed to be done, but put it out of my mind. "How long is the fair in town?" I asked.

"Four glorious days of all things crafty! Since I need a place to sleep, maybe I should go down there and snuggle up with a Pilgrim."

"I don't think she'd be their type," Heddy muttered behind me.

I swatted behind my back to hush her, and sighed. It was going to take a great deal of courage to form the words in my mouth. I thought about them for the longest time, hoping the earth would swallow me, but a cataclysmic event never happens when you need one most. "Miriam, you are welcome to stay at my house until something is available." Heddy slapped her head again and I turned to shush her.

"I've never been put into such a position before," Miriam said, peering inside her home. The sight made her sick and she put her hands over her face. "What am I going to do?"

"I just said you could stay at my house."

"I know what you said, Gloria! I'm trying to talk myself into it." I watched as Miriam peeked inside her doorway again, moaning. I felt like doing the same.

If Dalton heard the commotion out front, he never bothered to investigate. Miriam retrieved the suitcase from her trip out of the car trunk and stepped inside my house. She stopped at the sight. "Oh, my."

"We're helping Miss Glory put packages together for Christmas," Heddy said, making a path through the living room. "Just a few staples that everyone needs to . . ."

"I won't call you Miss Glory," Miriam said, turning to me. "That's a ridiculous name for a grown woman. During my stay, I will call you Gloria. Where do I put my valise?"

I kicked boxes aside with my foot and led Miriam to the den I had converted into another bedroom down the hall from the living room. Whiskers leaped from his perch on the bottom step and Miriam jumped. "Is that always inside?"

"Most of the time. He goes out to do his business but comes back when he's finished."

"Cats are simply rats with shorter noses," Miriam said, grumbling under her breath. I looked to Dalton and Heddy and they widened their eyes, lifting their hands as if defenseless to help. I waved my arm at them and sighed. It was going to be a long four days.

FOUR

The love of our neighbor in all its fullness
simply means being able to say to him,
"What are you going through?"
—Simone Weil

Chaz's new shift started at four the next day. The
store closed at nine, so there would only be five
hours when he'd have to deal with people. With the
exception of Larry and the rest of the janitorial team,
at night he'd have the place to himself to do what he
wanted. He wandered through Women's Clothing
and saw Ray there. He was pointing to a woman with
twins and pretending to gush over them. She pushed
the baby stroller closer to Chaz and he stopped. "Your
twins are really cute, Mrs. Grobinski." She beamed
and went into a story about Nicholas crawling but
how little Natalie was content to just watch her brother
do all the work. Mrs. Grobinski talked and talked and
Chaz was stuck. He didn't have the patience to be a

"courtesy officer." Ray saluted him and laughed his way into the men's department. Twenty minutes later Chaz carried Mrs. Grobinski's bags to the car and helped put the twins in their car seats.

He made his way to the mailroom and nosed through the letters still sitting in the bins from the afternoon mail. "It hasn't come," Kelly said.

He turned to see her standing in the door. She was pretty in an understated way. "Just curious," he said. "Hey, what if I'm not here when it comes? What will you do with it?"

She looked around the room and pointed to the top shelf. "I can put it right there under the air return."

Perfect. "That'd be great. Thanks." He turned to leave but stopped, looking at her. "You know, I don't come in until four and if that package comes early in the day maybe you could call me and I could come in and take a look at it."

"Sure."

"Or if you have the time, maybe you could bring it to my apartment?" He hadn't been with a woman since moving to town. He'd lived with a lot of women over the years but moved on when they felt compelled to change him.

She smiled and said she'd love to bring the package to his apartment.

When the dinner hour came, Miriam chose to remain in her room, where she had been since the day before. Heddy whispered throughout the evening, afraid of disturbing her. "It's all right," I said. "There's no need to walk on eggshells."

"Has she come out at all?" Heddy asked, whispering.

"I left this morning to take Marv Lichton to the doctor's office. Then Lakisha called and said Arianna was sick at school, so I picked her up and took her home. Maybe her royal highness broke out then."

"Did she eat anything?" Heddy said.

"I don't know. But if she gets thirsty I know where she can find some water." I laughed at myself and fell onto the sofa, pounding the cushions. The bedroom door opened down the hall and I put my finger to my lips, but cackled again when the door closed.

Miriam finally emerged from her room at eleven. She crept through the living room and turned off the porch light that was shining in her window. At eleven fifteen I walked downstairs and turned it back on. Miriam flicked it off again at eleven twenty. I was confident I could outlast her and had it shining bright at eleven thirty. Miriam crept through the living room at eleven forty-five.

"The light stays on, Miriam!"

Miriam screamed in the darkness. "It's shining into my bedroom," she said, digging her stubbed big toe into the carpet for comfort.

"Close the blinds and the drapes," I said.

"I have done that, but there is still a glowing beam making its way into my bedroom from that confounded light." She turned it off in a huff.

I forced my way next to her and flicked the light back on. "The light stays *on!*" Miriam clenched the robe in her hands and darted back to her room, slamming the door.

At midnight Chaz noticed a small figure dash beneath a rack of clothes in the juniors' department. A vacuum cleaner hummed behind him, but the young woman running it didn't notice he was there. He bent beneath the clothes and saw a small boy smiling at him. The young woman rushed beside Chaz and spoke in rapid Spanish to the boy, yanking him from beneath the clothes. She pulled him to the wall and made him sit up against it.

"He can't be in here," Chaz said, hoping she understood English.

"What are you going to do about it?" Her English was fine.

"They told me nobody can be in here. That's all I'm saying."

She was angry. "Miss Glory's got somebody at her house right now, so I didn't want to ask her to watch him." She was getting loud. "I got nowhere to take him tonight. If I don't bring him here, I lose this job." The little boy began to shrink beneath the clothes again, upset by his mother's voice.

Chaz rubbed his head. "How is that my problem?"

"You're making it your problem!" she said, flailing her arms. "He won't hurt nothing, and when I'm done we'll go home."

Chaz was getting angry. He had the potential to make some decent cash, and this woman was jeopardizing that for him. "He can't be up here," Chaz said. "He could break something and get hurt."

She lashed her arms toward him. "Then what do I do with him?"

Chaz didn't understand how her problem was

ending up on his shoulders or why he was responsible for her kid, but that's how it landed. "I'll take him into the security office. But don't bring him to work again." She watched as he led the little boy down the stairs.

"That's an ugly shirt," the boy said, eyeing the security uniform.

"Thanks, I like it, too," Chaz said.

"I didn't say I liked it. I said it was ugly."

"I know. That was sarcasm."

"What's sarcasm?"

"Never mind," Chaz said. "What's your name?"

The boy jumped down each stair, making a popping sound every time he landed. "Donovan. What's yours?"

Chaz opened the door to the office. "Chaz."

"That's a dumb name."

"Thanks."

"Hey, Raz," Donovan said, laughing.

The kid was getting on his last nerve. "It's Chaz."

"Okay, Spaz." This was the very reason Chaz had never liked children. Donovan saw leftover pizza sitting in a box on the desk and opened the lid. "Is this yours?" he asked, picking up a piece before Chaz could answer.

"Go ahead," Chaz said. "You can have that piece since you got finger smutz all over it." Donovan stood beside the desk and devoured the first piece, reaching for a second. "Didn't you eat dinner?" Donovan shook his head, and cheese dangled from his bottom lip onto his chin. He ran his shirtsleeve over his mouth. "I assume that's your mom out there working?" He nodded. "What's her name?"

"Mom," Donovan said.

"What do other people call her?"

The little boy shrugged.

"That's okay," Chaz said. "I'll find out later. I can tell she really likes me."

"No she don't," Donovan said, his mouth full.

"I know. That was sarcasm again. How old are you?"

Donovan held up five fingers. "How old are you?" he mumbled through a mouthful of pizza.

Chaz held up two fingers on one hand and four on the other. "Do you know how many that is?" Donovan shook his head. "Twenty-four."

"That's old. You're old," Donovan said.

"So far you've done wonders for my self-image," Chaz said. "Is your dad working tonight?" Donovan shrugged and took another bite. "Do you have a dad?"

Donovan shrugged again. "Some ass I've never met."

"You shouldn't say things like that," Chaz said.

"Why not? My mom says it all the time."

"Yeah, but it's not a word a little kid should say."

"Why not?" Donovan asked.

"Ask your mom."

"Why?"

This was going nowhere, and Chaz wanted more to drink than the two beers he had in his cup. "Forget it," Chaz said. He walked to the lockers and pulled out a blanket and pillow. "Why don't you lie down while your mom finishes up?"

Donovan hopped up on the desk. "I'm thirsty. I need some Coke," he said, snatching up the drink. Chaz lunged for it, but Donovan took a long sip and stuck out his tongue. "Gross. What is that?"

Chaz snatched up the drink. "It's nothing. Drink some water."

"I want Coke."

"A little kid shouldn't have Coke at midnight," Chaz said. "Even I know that." Chaz held the cup behind his back. "Do you want water?" Donovan shook his head. "All right, lie down there and I'll tell your mom you're in here." Donovan lay down and looked up at Chaz. "Do you know where you're at? You're in the security office, and if you get up off this couch every alarm in the building will ring. All I have to do is set the sequence into this superelectro pad." He pretended to punch numbers into a calculator on the desk, and Donovan lifted his head. "Nuh-uh. Just lie back down. I've got the numbers sequenced already. The alarms sound according to your body weight." Donovan looked puzzled and pulled the blanket up to his chin. Chaz turned off the light, leaving the one in the bathroom on. He stepped outside the office, waited a few minutes for movement, but there wasn't any. Donovan had fallen asleep. Chaz motioned to Donovan's mother, indicating that he was sleeping, and she nodded, continuing to vacuum. "Can't wait to work with you every night," he whispered to himself.

At one o'clock Donovan's mother came looking for him in the security office. "I can carry him to your car," Chaz said. "I'm Chaz. What's your name, by the way?" She looked him over without answering, and that angered him. "I just watched your kid for you. I think I should know your name."

"Carla," she snapped, flinging open the office door. Chaz picked Donovan up and his little arms dangled over his shoulders. Carla opened the back door to a Chevy Cavalier. "Does he have a special seat or something?" Chaz whispered. She shook her head and he sat Donovan in the backseat, wrapping a seat belt around him. His head wobbled and his eyes opened. "Go back to sleep," Chaz said.

"Good night, Spaz."

Chaz got his foot out of the way before Carla drove away. "You're welcome," he said, shouting at the back of the car.

He finished his rounds, and just before two A.M. did the final lockdown. He changed back into his jeans and sweatshirt and left his uniform in the locker before pulling a hat down over his ears for the walk home. He walked through the town square; it was fully decorated for Christmas, including the three fir trees that lit up the night. Just past the square, in front of the library, he noticed a man sleeping on a bench with his arms wrapped around himself. Chaz stopped when he recognized him as Mike, the young homeless man he'd met in front of Wilson's. He wondered how he could sleep out in the cold, and stood watching him for the longest time. He shook his head and walked toward his apartment. He was freezing.

The air stabbed at his lungs and he coughed when

he breathed in. He walked past a row of houses that were still dark at this time of early morning, but stopped when he saw a woman holding a small child in front of an upstairs window. A man laid his hand on the boy's back and leaned in to kiss his forehead. Chaz remembered his own father getting up in the middle of the night when he was sick as a boy. He couldn't do much more than his mother was already doing, but he was there patting Chaz's back and telling bad jokes. Nausea rose to his throat and he hurried down the street.

He collapsed onto the futon and opened a can of beer. The Christmas lights from across the street lit up the apartment. Why didn't those people turn them off when they went to bed like everybody else? He drew the blinds but the lights bored their way through the cracks. He hated those lights and the people who owned the house. He hated his apartment and the fact that nothing—*nothing*—ever changed in his life. It just took place in a different town with a different job and different women. He thought about that, and also about Donovan, and Mike sleeping on the bench, and drank till he passed out.

FIVE

Too often we underestimate the power of a touch, a smile,
a kind word, a listening ear, an honest compliment,
or the smallest act of caring, all of which have the
potential to turn a life around.
—Leo Buscaglia

A slow-moving road plow was in front of me, and I followed it as long as my patience would allow before opting for another route downtown. I made the turn onto Oakdale and noticed a very pregnant young woman on the sidewalk pulling a suitcase with one hand and holding another one under her arm. I passed her but watched in the rearview mirror as she struggled to pull the suitcase. "What in the world?" I said, stopping the car. "Why is she walking around in this weather?" The woman was petite, with unruly shoulder-length blond hair. I watched through the back window as she struggled to keep the mane out of her face. The small suitcase she was holding dropped from under her arm and she squatted to pick up the bag. I peered through the passenger window trying to see if she was heading for a car or bus stop. "What is she doing?" I mumbled as I threw the car in reverse. I backed up alongside the young woman and rolled down the window. "Do you need help getting those somewhere?"

Tears fell down her face. "I don't know where I'm going. The landlord kicked me out of my apartment."

I pushed the button for the trunk and jumped out of the car, grabbing her bags. "Let me take you somewhere. Why were you kicked out?"

She put her hand on her belly and watched as I put her suitcase inside the trunk. "I haven't paid rent in two and a half months. I told him I was going to try to find another roommate because I can't pay it myself, but I can't find anybody else. Men showed up this morning to rip out the carpeting and paint the walls."

The wind picked up and I motioned for her to get in the car. "Tell you what," I said. "I live just down the street. Maybe you could call your parents."

She shook her head. "They're divorced," she said. "My dad's out west and I haven't seen him since I was thirteen. My mom's an hour north but she's the reason I moved here in the first place. We haven't spoken a whole lot in the last five months."

"Any friends nearby where I can drop you?"

"No."

I wasn't accustomed to asking strangers to sleep at my house, but how could I just leave a pregnant woman without a home to wander the streets? I could see the headlines: Pregnant Woman Dies of Exposure After Woman Passes Her By on the Way to Lunch. "You can sleep at my house if you like. Maybe tomorrow things will look different." She blew her nose and nodded.

My living room was small but warm, with a fireplace on the far wall and an upright piano in front of another. The walls were a shade of green, and at the top, a border with ducks on it stretched around the room. I love ducks and had put the border up myself. The carpet was a soft pile, the color of a rose. The young woman was uncomfortable, her arms crossed in front of her.

"I hate this carpeting," I said, dropping the suitcase to the floor. "Please. Feel free to sit." I motioned to the sofa. She sat down and sank into the green cushions. "Who puts pink carpeting in a living room?" I said. "When I moved in I said I'd change it, but it's cheaper to cover the walls than the floor. Of course some people might say, 'Who paints their walls green and tops them off with ducks when they have pink carpeting?' All those interior designers on TV would just cringe." My Christmas tree was in front of the window, decorated with a hodgepodge of bulbs and beads. "We really should get acquainted," I said, sitting in my favorite chair, a dark leather recliner with patch-worn arms. "I'm Gloria Bailey, and I live here alone. I have seven grandchildren that I adore. They're brilliant, as you can imagine. My—" A door opened, and I winced. For a moment I had forgotten about Miriam. I looked up and saw her standing in the hall doorway.

"Who is this?" Miriam asked, walking in front of the young woman. "Who are you?"

"I'm Erin."

"I see you have a suitcase, Erin. Are you going to the airport?" Erin shook her head. Miriam eyeballed her. "Are you a military wife?" Erin shook her head again. "Where is the father of that child you're carrying?"

I stood up in an effort to save the poor girl. "I've asked Erin to stay here for the night," I said.

Miriam turned on me. "Here? Are you running a boardinghouse, Gloria? I'm cramped as it is in these small quarters."

The hairs on my neck stood on end, and I positioned myself between Miriam and Erin, whispering in that too-loud-to-be-considered-whispering voice, "This is my home, Miriam, and I'll ask whomever I want, whenever I want, to stay in it." I turned to Erin. "This is my neighbor Miriam, who's staying with me for a few days." Erin attempted to smile but Miriam was ignoring her anyway. "Why don't you sit down, Miriam, and let's enjoy a visit with Erin."

Miriam crossed her arms and sulked, reading a plaque I kept on the wall next to the fireplace.

May those who love us, love us.
And those that don't love us
May God turn their hearts:
And if He does not turn their hearts,
May He turn their ankles
So we'll know them by their limping.

Miriam shook her head and moved farther away from me.

I smiled at Erin and sat down. "Just to put your mind at ease—I'm not a psychopath. Are you?"

She laughed. "No."

"Good. The jury's still out about Miriam but

maybe we'll all manage to sleep through the night." I attempted to tilt the recliner back, and Whiskers bolted from underneath it up the stairs. Miriam growled at the sight of him. "That was Whiskers. My roommate. He's afraid of his own shadow *and* my grandson's brown toy horse, Pink. Whiskers is terrified of Pink. I have no idea why. I've tried to get Whiskers counseling, but this is clearly something he needs to work through on his own." She smiled and I leaned back in the recliner, resting my hands on my stomach. "I've blabbed on long enough. You're probably still freezing. Would you like something warm to drink?" Erin nodded. "Miriam, can I get you something to drink?"

"No," Miriam said, an icy chill filling the living room as she sighed.

I got up and walked to the kitchen. "When are you due?"

"Four more weeks," Erin said.

I popped a mug full of water into the microwave and pulled out a package of cocoa mix from a drawer, shaking it. "Is this your first baby?"

"Yes."

"Are you married?" Miriam asked. Erin shook her head. "Where is the father?"

"I'm not sure," Erin said.

Miriam made a long, grinding noise at the back of her throat and stepped closer to the sofa. "I see."

"Will you be keeping the baby?" I said, leaning into the doorway.

"I want to, but . . . I don't know."

I walked back into the kitchen and Erin spoke louder. "My boyfriend bolted after he found out I was pregnant," she said. "He just up and left town."

"Well, he's not exactly top-drawer, is he?" Miriam said, sitting. "Men are horrible creatures. They're all the same, I'm afraid."

"That's not true," I said, calling out from the kitchen.

"Well, yes, I agree," Miriam said. "My first husband was horrible. An actor. A horrible actor, I might add. His mother was worse, a horrendous person with the face of a hawk. But my second husband was pure gold. An English professor. We met when he brought two of his classes to see a play I was in. We had a lovely marriage, but then he took it upon himself to die and leave me a widow at forty-seven."

"When did he pass away?" Erin asked.

"Four years ago."

I coughed and choked in the kitchen, leaning onto the counter for support. "Are you okay, Gloria?" Erin asked, leaning over to see me inside the kitchen.

"Something was hard to swallow," I said.

"Things blew up with my mother when she found out I was pregnant," Erin said. "She put me through college by herself. She can't believe I let this happen."

"Does she know you're in town?" Miriam asked.

Erin nodded. "We haven't talked much, though. I moved here and was living with my best friend from college. I didn't have anyplace else to go. But a couple of months ago her boyfriend moved to Colorado for his job and she followed him there."

"Leaving you to pay the rent alone," Miriam said. She shook her head, slapping her thighs. "You can't trust anyone anymore. Remember that next time. You can't even trust—"

I popped my head inside the living room, talking over Miriam. "And you have no idea where your boyfriend is?"

"I've tried to find him through former employers and the Internet, but haven't had any luck."

"He's a ninny and a dolt," Miriam said. "A worthless combination."

I topped Miriam's voice as I took the cup out of the microwave. "Was he a serious boyfriend, or just . . ." I let my voice trail off.

"I thought we were serious," Erin said, her voice rising. "You can see what he thought of me. How stupid am I?"

I poured cocoa into the mug and stirred it, adding marshmallows to the top. "You're not stupid." I handed the cup to Erin and sat beside her. "You just wanted to believe in love. Who doesn't want that?"

Erin shook her head. "Not him. Not any guy today."

Mike was in front of Wilson's again when Chaz arrived for work. He saw Chaz coming but stayed put, leaning against the wall. "Chaz."

"Hi, Mike," Chaz said.

"Don't worry. I'm not loitering."

Chaz laughed and walked toward the entrance. "Where are you from? Kentucky? Georgia? I can't tell."

"Somewhere around there."

"Do you work anywhere?" Chaz asked.

"Sometimes. The industrial plant needs help once a week unloading a shipment. A few of us show up and they pay us that day. It gets me through the week. I don't need much." His beard was thicker than it had been earlier in the week, and Chaz noticed dirt in the creases around his eyes. He wondered where he showered.

"How long have you been . . ."

"On the street?" Mike said. "Six or seven years. It's easy to lose track."

"Does your family know where you are?"

Mike shook his head and blew into his hands; a small puff of smoke spread out in front of him. "Better that way." He shoved his hands in his pockets and watched Chaz shift from one foot to the other. "You don't have to try to say anything."

Chaz opened the door to Wilson's and for the first time in years wished he *did* have something to say.

"Four to six weeks! You must be mad!" I stuck my head out of the bedroom at the same time that Erin did. We looked at each other from across the hall and listened to Miriam. I strained to see my watch and groaned; it was too early in the morning to be listening to more of Miriam's drama. "I did hear you, but how long could it possibly take to rip up floorboards, replace carpeting, and hang new drywall?" We crept down the stairs and saw Miriam cradling the phone. She looked haggard and worn. "It's destroyed," she said. "Some of it can be saved, but most of it has too much water damage."

For the first time in our relationship I felt something other than aversion for Miriam. "I'm so sorry," I said.

"Insurance will cover two weeks in a hotel, but who wants to stay in one of the hotels around here?"

I couldn't believe what I was about to say. "You could stay here."

She threw her hands in the air. "My life couldn't get any worse than it is right now."

I turned to go back upstairs. "Well then, breakfast is promptly at seven thirty and dinner is at six," I said. "If you live here you are expected not only to eat the meals but also to help prepare and clean up after said meals."

"I don't—"

I didn't let her finish. "You are also expected to clean up after yourself and keep sarcastic remarks to a minimum." I closed my bedroom door and wondered what I had gotten myself into now.

Donovan ran into the security office at nine thirty that evening. "Miss Glory has two women living with her right now," Carla said to Chaz. "I don't know what else to do with him."

Chaz shrugged and pointed to the sofa. "He can sleep here till you're done." Carla kissed the top of Donovan's head and went to work.

"What are you eating, Spaz?" Donovan said, running to the desk. Chaz handed him part of his peanut butter and jelly sandwich. "Peanut butter?" Donovan said. He took a bite. "We need to pack something else for work."

"Then your mom should pack you something," Chaz said. "It's her job, anyway." Chaz handed him a packaged cupcake.

"Oh, yeah!" Donovan said, smiling. "That's what I'm talking about." He danced like he'd just caught a ball in the end zone, and raised his hand over his head. "Up high." Chaz slapped his hand. "On the side." Chaz slapped it again. "Down low." Donovan pulled his hand away before Chaz could slap it. "Too slow." He reared his head back, laughing. His jokes were corny and he drove Chaz crazy with all his babbling, but in a strange way Chaz actually liked the kid's company.

"You got a Christmas tree?" Donovan asked, picking apart the cupcake.

"No. Do you?"

"No. But Miss Glory gave my mom a big bush with little ormanants on it." Donovan shoved a bite of cupcake into his mouth. "I told her Santa won't leave presents under a bush, but Miss Glory said some children on the other side of the world don't even have a Christmas bush. Is that true?"

Chaz poured hot coffee into a foam cup. "Yeah, that's right."

"What do they have? Like a flower or a piece of corn or something?"

"I don't know," Chaz said. "But I bet they come up with something that works."

"What do you use?" Donovan asked.

"Nothing. I don't really do Christmas."

"Why not?" Donovan said. "Don't you believe in Santa Claus?" He was wide-eyed and bewildered at the thought of it.

"I believe in the spirit of Santa Claus," Chaz said. "Who wouldn't?"

"Maybe you could come over to my house and see if Santa leaves you something under my Christmas bush. He knows you'll be there because he knows everything."

Chaz hadn't celebrated Christmas with anyone in years and couldn't imagine what that would be like anymore. "I've got plans for that day, but thanks, though."

Donovan ran to the video monitors and shoved the last of the cupcake into his mouth. "Take me to Santa's toy shop."

"No," Chaz said. "You're not supposed to be on the floor."

"I won't be on the floor," Donovan said, prancing. "I'll be in Santa's toy shop." He grabbed on to Chaz's hand, pulling it. "Come on. Just show me."

There wasn't any point in talking Donovan out of it because he'd just run there when Chaz wasn't looking. Larry, Carla, and Monique were busy cleaning other areas of the store and didn't notice Donovan dashing through Children's Clothing to get to the Toy Department. His eyes lit up when he saw the small red workshop with a marshmallow roof splattered with gumdrops, frosting shutters, and a chocolate-bar door. Lollipops sprang out of the garden around the building, gingerbread men clung to the sides, and the door handle was a giant candy cane. Donovan burst through the door and frowned when he saw an empty workshop put together with plywood and two-by-fours. "Where's the toys?"

"Santa can't make stuff here," Chaz said. "Look how small this is. He just comes here to find out what kids want; then he sends those orders up to, you know, his elves."

Donovan closed the door and sat on the floor, disappointed. "Did you come here today and tell Santa what you want?"

"No," Chaz said.

"If I worked here I'd tell him that I want toys that are fun to play with," Donovan said, kicking the door open and closed with his feet. "No dumb stuff! And for my mom to get some press-on nails that she's been wanting. And I'd tell him I want a dad."

Chaz wasn't good at this sort of thing and looked at his watch. "Come on, let's go. It's late."

Donovan pushed open the small white gate and followed him. "Do you want to play Superman or Spider-Man tonight?"

"Spider-Man, but only for a few minutes," Chaz said. "You need to sleep."

"But my eyes are still open," Donovan said. "Look." He craned his neck up for Chaz to see.

"Yeah, I know. But they should be closed. You're just a little kid."

"I'm tall inside."

Chaz sighed. Why did he continue to argue with a five-year-old? They walked into the security office and Chaz pointed to a video monitor in horror. "The dreaded Snake Eye McQueen is stealing the Housewares Department blind. What'll we do?"

Donovan jumped onto the desk and pretended to scale the wall. "I'll save you." He jumped off the desk and flailed about with an imaginary culprit before tying the thief up and leaving him in the middle of the room.

Chaz made him lie down on the couch and Donovan grabbed his hand. "Are you kind of like my dad?"

It felt like a sock to Chaz's stomach. How could Donovan think of some guy who gave him a peanut butter sandwich as his dad? "No. I'm nothing like a dad," Chaz said.

"You could be a dad," Donovan said.

"No, I couldn't." Nothing in his life would qualify as father material.

"Can I always sleep here?"

Chaz stood at the side of the couch; he needed to shut this conversation down. "No," he said. "Your mom has to find somebody to watch you at night because I won't be staying here forever."

Donovan sat up. "Where are you going?"

"I don't know," Chaz said. "Somewhere, though. I'm just trying to make enough money so I can get there."

Donovan turned his back to him and pulled the blanket up to his neck. "My mom said men always leave."

Chaz had no idea what to say, so he left him alone. He thought about a beer and glanced at his watch: four hours to go. Carla caught him closing the door. She was wearing pink scrubs for work. "Go in if you want," Chaz said. "I just turned off the light." She shook her head and turned to go. "Carla." She stopped and he wondered what he would talk to her about. "Donovan's a good kid." She nodded. Chaz hadn't noticed how small she was, maybe just a hair over five feet. Her face looked sallow and worn, the circles under her eyes actually darker than the eyes. Maybe if her black hair was down around her face it would soften her features, but every time he'd seen her it was held back in a tight ponytail. "He's funny and seems really smart," he said.

She headed for the back stairs leading to the service entrance. "He doesn't get it from me," she said. "He doesn't even look like me."

A metal light with a huge bulb hung over the door, lighting the back entrance. They stood in the silence at the top of the stairs while she smoked. A foggy gray ribbon circled her head. "Is Donovan's dad here?" Chaz asked. She nodded. "Does he see Donovan?"

"He doesn't care."

Chaz crossed his arms to keep warm. "How could anybody not care for Donovan?" That came out quicker than he expected.

She looked at him, and her face softened for the first time since he'd known her. "You don't look like you're from here," she said.

"Where do I look like I'm from?"

She shrugged. "Any place but here."

"I've lived in a lot of places," Chaz said.

"You don't want to be in one spot too long."

"Seems that way."

She took a long drag and blew smoke toward the light. "That way nobody ever gets to know you and you don't have to know anybody, either." He smiled but didn't say anything. "Where's your family?" she said.

"My parents are dead. I was an only child."

She nodded. "Do you miss them?"

"This time of year, especially. Donovan said he wants to tell Santa you want press-on nails for Christmas."

She laughed and leaned against the metal railing, blowing smoke up into the air. "Did you have Christmas with your parents as a kid?"

"Yeah. Sure," he said.

"Did you get lots of presents?"

He blew into his hands. "Not too many. Enough, though."

"Like what?" she asked. "What was one of your favorites?"

He leaned against the door. "I used to love Hot Wheels cars, and one year they gave me the racetrack. I can't remember anything else I got that year because for months that racetrack was all I talked about." He shoved his hands in his pockets. "I took the track to the basement and I put it together in the shape of an oval." He laughed at the thought. "Oh, the imagination and vision I had! Dad came down and helped me make it into the shape of a figure eight with all the cool ramps and loops."

"When did he die?" Carla said.

"Just a year or two after that."

She nodded and inhaled. "When I was little I wished that my old man would come around at Christmas. He'd bring me presents and put all the ones that said 'assembly required' together for me, you know, like your dad did. Then we'd eat a huge turkey and he'd play with me all day." She twisted the cigarette butt into the railing and pulled out another smoke, flipping it up and down in the palm of her hand.

"Did he ever come around?" Chaz asked.

She put the end of the cigarette into her mouth. "Gave me a Frisbee. Unwrapped. I was so excited. I asked him to play hide-and-go-seek and he hid behind the couch. I found him right away and then ran off to hide in the hall closet. He never bothered to look for me. I heard the front door close." She put the unlit cigarette back into the pack. "All my life I just wanted him to notice that I was there. How the hell could he notice me when he couldn't even pretend to find me?" She took the cigarette back out of the pack and lit it.

They were quiet as wind carried a cloud of smoke into his face. "Hey," Chaz said. "I'm not sure how long I'm going to be working here at night, so . . ."

She turned to look at him, taking a drag. "Do you think you can find anybody to watch Donovan?"

She took another puff and flicked the cigarette off the loading ramp before opening the door. "I need to ask Miss Glory but she's been busy with lots of people at her house," she said. "I don't have any place else. Once somebody finds out he's here I'll get fired. That's how it goes." She disappeared up the stairs and he heard a vacuum kick on.

Chaz peeked through the security office window. Carla had to find a place for Donovan soon. He was getting too close, and that was making Chaz uncomfortable.

SIX

> One learns people through the heart,
> not the eyes or the intellect.
> —Mark Twain

As always, Marshall Wilson agreed to help provide hats, socks, and mittens for the Christmas packages Heddy and Dalton and I were putting together. "Any big Christmas plans?" he asked as I gathered my purse and coat in his office.

"No," I said. "All my kids are spending it with their in-laws this year. I'll go to Dalton and Heddy's. How about you?"

He pulled a picture out of his wallet and handed it to me. "That's my grandson. He's been in Japan at an air base there. His grandmother and I haven't seen him in two years."

I studied the dark eyes staring back at me in the photo as Marshall talked on. "Are you all right, Gloria?"

I looked at the picture again. "Yes. His face reminds me of my Matthew, that's all. He's very handsome," I said, handing the photo back to him.

I left his office, thinking. There had been so many faces over the years. A pang cut through my heart as it always did when I saw someone who reminded me of Matt. I pushed through the front doors and dropped my purse on the sidewalk. I moaned as the contents scattered, a tube of lipstick rolling beneath a car. I knelt on the pavement, peering under it. "My favorite shade, too. Wouldn't you know?" I said, stretching for the tube. "No way I'm leaving Morning Rose behind." I took off my boot and swiped at the tube, grunting with each stretch. Finally, I flung my purse and used it to drag the tube back to me. I brushed the dusting of snow off my clothes and blew strands of hair out of my eyes. I was way past due for a trim. I felt around my head for the missing bobby pin and pinned the stray hairs back.

Once I had everything together, I got in my car and pulled away from the curb but stopped when I saw Robert Layton getting out of his SUV in front of his office next door. "Robert!" I said, yelling out the passenger-side window and honking the horn.

He closed the office door and stepped to the car

window. "Morning, Glory!" He laughed, stomping snow off his shoes.

"When I saw you I realized that you *can* help," I said.

He leaned over to hear better. "What's that?"

"If I hadn't dropped my purse I would have missed you entirely. Don't they call that serendipity?" He looked confused but I barreled on. "I have a girl who needs work."

He pretended to collapse inside the window. "I was that close to my office door and a quick getaway." He raised his head and looked at me. "The last time I gave one of your girls work she stole my printer, my office chair, *and* my favorite pen. I'm still not over it. I loved that pen!"

I leaned toward him. "I feel bad about that; I really do," I said. "Sometimes they're ready to make a change and sometimes they're not. She wasn't ready."

"Thanks for telling me *now*!"

"But this girl is different," I said. Robert opened and closed his hand as if holding a puppet; he'd heard all that before. "She's very mature for her age." Robert gestured for me to keep laying it on thick. "She has another mouth to feed and the father is nowhere to be found."

"There it is!" he said. "There's the kicker." He

sighed and waved at someone on the street, thinking. "Is she a big-boned girl? Does she look like she could haul off a desk or maybe the conference table?"

I slapped the steering wheel. "She's a petite little thing," I said. "No bigger than a minute."

Robert ran his thumb over the passenger-side mirror, clearing away the snow and dirt, then held up his hands. "All right, Gloria. I'll give one of your girls another shot." I clapped my hands together. "I need someone to help Jodi on a part-time basis with phones and filing. She'll have to answer to Jodi and you know how she is. She's a much tougher boss than I am. If her pen comes up missing she'll get a bloodhound after your girl."

I reached over to shake Robert's hand. "Deal! Can I have her call Jodi right away?" He nodded, defeated. "You won't regret this, Robert," I said. "She'll be perfect for your office and she won't take a thing."

He backed away from the car, bending over to see inside. "Promise?"

"No," I said, laughing, and pulled away.

It was snowing when Chaz walked to work that afternoon. Large flakes collected on the sidewalk and he hurried toward Wilson's. It was getting colder each day. The weather people spouted that it was the coldest weather in ten years and the roads were constantly freezing. He saw Mike sitting in the middle of the town square but it was too late to pretend he hadn't seen him. He threw up his hand and waved. No matter what Chaz did, it seemed that guy was always around reminding him of how cold it was outside.

Although it was going to take longer, he chose to walk around the square instead of through it so he could avoid Mike. He kept his head down and hurried for the store. Chaz recognized the guy in front of Wilson's talking with someone in a car. On several occasions Chaz had seen him going into the building next door. He was a lawyer or something. The car drove away and Chaz crossed the street. "Hey," the lawyer said. Chaz nodded and walked through the front door. He noticed a girl off in the corner. She was behind the sales rack in Women's Clothing and her blond hair caught his eye. She kept pushing it behind her ear but it would fall again, and she'd cock her head just so to keep it in place. Fred Clauson stepped to his side and briefed him on a couple of late-night deliveries. Chaz listened but kept his eye on her. She was the most beautiful girl he'd seen since moving to town. He couldn't see the rest of her body behind the clothes rack, but knew it had to be as beautiful as her face. He didn't approach her, reasoning she wouldn't be interested, and followed Fred to the security office.

Erin walked into the kitchen and opened her arms. "Will this work? I found it on sale at Wilson's." She was wearing black maternity pants with a purple blousy top.

"Work for what?" Miriam asked.

"I bought it thinking I'd be going on interviews this week," Erin said. "But Gloria found a job for me today."

"It's perfect," I said, banging a spoon on the side of a pot.

"But women who work in law offices on TV are always wearing suits," Erin said.

"You're dressed fine," I said to Erin. "You're not going to court. Besides, Robert Layton gave up on suits years ago."

Miriam sat slumped in a chair at the table, looking at her house. For days men had been ripping out carpeting and tearing out damaged walls while setting her belongings on the driveway. When she came in each evening she was exhausted and miserable from sorting through the things she had collected during her marriage to Lynn. On more than one occasion I offered to help but it was something she needed to do alone, painstakingly going through bloated photo albums or cards and letters that were blurry with ink and salvaging what she could.

When she stepped into her home men would escort her back out. "We can't have you in here," the contractor would say. "Please, it's for your safety." Miriam would charge through anyway, telling the crew how to do their work.

Early one morning I answered the door and found one of the crewmen looking sheepish. "I'm sorry to bother you, ma'am," he said. "But would you mind keeping your friend out of her house?"

I felt bad for him. "I'm afraid that's like keeping a rash from spreading," I said.

There was no expression on his face. "Great. Thanks." He went back to his work and I leaned out the door to hear Miriam barking orders from inside her home.

"I always told Lynn I wanted a different house,"

Miriam had said earlier in the week. "Now I want it, but it's ruined." I tried to encourage her, pointing out that now she could put up new walls with new color and paper; she could even make rooms bigger or smaller, but if there was a silver lining Miriam wouldn't see it.

She moaned and strained to read a stained-glass plaque hanging in my window:

Grant me the senility to forget the people I never liked anyway
The good fortune to run into the ones I do
And the eyesight to tell the difference

She grunted, shaking her head, and I laughed, watching her. I pulled plates down from a cupboard and held them in front of her. She sighed like a horse and stood wearily to her feet. "Don't be late," Miriam scolded. "Employers have no patience for tardiness."

I rolled my eyes and dumped mashed potatoes into a bowl. "She won't be late."

"And they won't tolerate any mucking around, either," Miriam said. "Remember that."

I handed the potatoes to Erin while I pulled a meat loaf from the oven. Miriam frowned when she saw it but brightened when I slid a pan full of hot rolls from the top rack. I poured peas into a bowl and handed them to Erin. "Have you told your mother that you're here?"

"Not yet," she said. Miriam sighed, shaking her head, and Erin pretended not to notice.

I filled three glasses with ice and opened the fridge for the pitcher of tea. "You can invite her to come visit," I said. "I could fix dinner and the two of you could talk about what you need to do." Erin was quiet, taking the drinks to the table. She wasn't enthused about that idea. "When the time's right."

"But the time better be soon by the looks of your belly," Miriam said.

I hissed at Miriam and sat, patting Erin's hand. "Just ignore her. My grandson taught me this. He'll throw up his little hand and say, 'Talk to the hand, Grandma.' So just throw your hand up when she talks."

"I can hear you, Gloria," Miriam said. "I'm sitting right here."

I ate my food with one hand and raised the other, putting it in front of Miriam. "Talk to the hand, Miriam." I leaned close to Erin. "Whatever happened between you and your mother, I'm sure she's over it and just wants to see you again. And nothing will be able to keep her from that little one you're carrying." Erin nodded, moving the food around on her plate. "If you're open to it, I think you should give me your mother's name and phone number . . . just in case something happens." I reached behind me and pulled out a pad and pen from the telephone table and slid it in front of Erin. After a while she jotted down a name and number and moved the pad to the side of my plate. I slipped the paper inside my jacket pocket and jumped up from the table. "Oh, my! I almost forgot." I dug through my purse and handed a set of car keys to Erin. "These are for you."

"I can't take your car, Gloria," Erin said. "You need it. I'll take the bus to work."

"These aren't keys to my car," I said. "They're keys to your car. The Silver Fox." I pushed open the drapes at the kitchen window.

"But you need it for one of your families," she said.

"You're one of my families now," I said. "When you can get a car of your own you'll give it back to me and I'll pass it on."

"Does it have seat belts?" Miriam asked, peering out the window.

"Of course it has seat belts!"

Erin stammered for something to say. "I can't . . ."

"Jack said she was good as new," I said. "And she is. I took her for a spin myself." I pointed to her chair. "Sit down and eat before it gets cold." We sat and ate together, three women who had been plopped into each other's lives in the strangest of circumstances, and though there were several gaps and silences, the conversation was civil. *Very civil*, I thought. Maybe things were finally on an upward swing.

Chaz was in the security office monitoring the video screens when he noticed shoppers scrambling for the front doors. He ran up the stairs and saw the lawyer from next door on the other side of the street crouched down on the ground beside a car that had smashed into a light pole. Ray was also out there; he had run out when he heard a bang that rattled the store windows. Chaz saw the driver of the car standing and talking, so he didn't think the accident was more than a fender bender. "He hasn't moved," a woman said, watching the scene.

Chaz caught a glimpse of Mike on the ground and felt himself shrinking backward. Two hours before he had avoided Mike. He felt his hand shaking and grabbed on to it with his other hand. Paramedics jumped out of an ambulance and seemed to take forever getting Mike onto a stretcher. "He still isn't moving," the woman said again. Chaz walked to the back of the store and ran out the service entrance for home.

The phone rang thirty minutes later and Chaz let it ring. A few minutes later it rang again and he picked it up. "What happened?" Ray said.

"I got sick," Chaz said, lying.

"Did you see what happened out front?"

"Some of it." He sat down. "Is that guy okay?"

"I don't know," Ray said. "He was pretty banged up." Chaz felt his hand shaking again and walked to the refrigerator, pulling out a beer. "Do you think you'll come back in?"

"I can't," Chaz said. "I'm really sick."

"All right. We'll get it covered."

"Thanks," Chaz said. He was about to hang up when he thought of Donovan. What would happen to him if Ray or Fred covered his shift? "Ray," he said, shouting into the phone. "I'll come in later."

"You sure?"

"I'll be there by nine," Chaz said. He warmed up

some macaroni and cheese and drank two beers while sitting at the card table. The sun was setting but he didn't turn on the lights; he was used to the dark. He called information, got the number for the hospital, and dialed it before he forgot it. No one would give him any information. Why would they? He didn't even know Mike's last name.

"Are you a family member?" the woman asked him. He tried to explain that Mike didn't have any family and that he talked to Mike all the time, but none of that mattered.

He lay down on the futon but his mind played the scene over and over again. As soon as he'd feel himself drifting he'd see Mike's body and jump awake. What if Mike died? What if he died and his parents never knew about it? How would they live the rest of their lives without knowing what had happened to him? The obnoxious Christmas lights from across the street streamed into his room and he covered his head.

When the phone rang at eight he grabbed for it. It was Kelly at Wilson's. "The package came," she said. A long pause followed. "I see you're not working tonight. Would you like me to bring it to you when I get off?" Chaz felt every nerve inside his body and he sat on the edge of the futon, rubbing his head. "Chaz? Do you still want me to bring it to you?"

He couldn't let her come. He just couldn't do it this time. "No."

She fumbled for something to say. "Well, what do you want me to—"

"I don't care," he said.

She was quiet on the other end; then the line went dead.

Carla crept to the door and opened it, keeping an eye on Thomas as she pulled it closed. "Where are you going?" Thomas said.

She jumped at his voice. "I need to check on Donovan," she said.

He rolled over, watching her. "He's fine. Get back in bed."

"He's been alone a long time," Carla said, whispering. "I'll be right back."

"Two minutes," Thomas said, leaning up on his elbow.

She stepped across the hall to Donovan's room and locked his door behind her. She knew a lock wouldn't keep Thomas out, but it was all she could do. Donovan was watching TV like she'd asked him to do when Thomas arrived. She sat down next to him and he jumped in her lap, making her flinch. The bruises on her legs were tender. "I need you to get dressed," she whispered, pulling a pair of pants off the end of his bed.

"Why?"

"Shh," she said, helping him into the pants. "I need to take you to Miss Glory's tonight."

"Why?" he said, struggling to get a sweatshirt over his head.

"Because you shouldn't stay here tonight," she said, tying his sneakers.

"Why not?"

She held his hand and put her finger to her lips. "Stop asking questions and be quiet." She turned the doorknob and slowly pulled back the door, creeping into the hallway with Donovan. She grabbed her coat off the rack by the front door and dragged Donovan to her car.

Dalton, Heddy, Erin, and I dumped out several garbage bags and sorted through the clothing inside. Each winter I found bags of clothing sitting on the porch, but this year there seemed to be more than ever. We threw away the clothing that was too tattered to be usable and made piles of nice, warm clothes we could include in some of the packages we were making. Miriam never offered to help. She sat at the kitchen window, staring at the huge construction Dumpster that was sitting in her driveway.

The doorbell rang at eight thirty. I took huge steps over the piles of clothing and opened the door a crack, smiling when I saw Donovan. "Hola!" I said, unlatching the chain lock.

"Hola!" he said, marching past me.

Carla stood on the porch with her back to the door. "Carla?" I said, stepping outside.

She wiped her face, turning to me. "I'm in a bind tonight, Miss Glory. I'm going to work but don't have anyone to watch Donovan. I know you have all these people staying with you, but is it okay if he stays over?"

"Sure." I studied Carla's face. "Are you all right?"

Carla nodded. "I'm just cold and worried that I wouldn't have a place for him, you know. I need to run or I'll be late." She leaned her head inside the doorway, kissing Donovan. "Be a good boy for Miss Glory. Yes?" He nodded and she walked past me down the steps. I watched her get inside the car and then shut the front door behind me.

"Who's this?" Miriam asked as I hung Donovan's coat on the hall tree.

"This," I said, proudly, "is Donovan, a longtime friend of mine. Isn't that right?" I held up my hand and he gave me a high five.

Miriam eyed the small suitcase. "Is he staying here?"

"For the night."

"There isn't any more room," she said. "Look at this place. It's an absolute mess. This rubbish needs to be taken to the street for the rag and bone man, but you're bringing another person in on top of all of it!"

I jerked straight and felt the curls bounce around on top of my head. "Go to your room, Miriam." Dalton, Heddy, and Erin pretended to be knee-deep in clothes.

"I am not a child, Gloria!"

"Then stop acting like one."

Miriam slammed the door to her room and I sighed. There was just no way to bridge the gap between us.

.   .   .

Chaz packed an extra sandwich and showed up for work at nine, just as Ray was leaving. "Has anybody heard anything about Mike?" he asked.

"I haven't heard anything," Ray said, glancing at him. "You don't look so good. Why don't you just go home? The store can go one night without somebody on duty."

Chaz set the plastic grocery bag that contained his dinner on the desk. "I need the money," he said.

"I hear that." Ray zipped up his coat. "I talked with my wife and we'd like to have you over for Christmas dinner. You up for that?"

Chaz hung up his coat and closed the locker. Ray needed to get out before Donovan came racing through the door. "I'm eating with some relatives that day."

"I didn't think you had any family," Ray said.

"I have an aunt about ninety minutes from here."

Ray threw a backpack over his shoulder. "Just making sure. Didn't want you to spend Christmas alone." He clapped Chaz on the back and left.

Chaz watched the monitors and saw the janitorial team working in Menswear, Juniors', and the housewares department. The two outside monitors showed Carla getting out of her car at the loading dock entrance. Chaz spread out the sandwich and chips for Donovan. After several minutes Chaz walked up the stairs to the main floor, looking for him. Carla was pushing her cart outside the ladies' restroom and he caught her before she went inside. She was wearing small headphones on her ears and didn't see him. He touched her arm and she flinched. She looked terrible. "Hey!" he said. "Where's Donovan?"

She took one headphone away from her ear. "Miss Glory could watch him tonight." She snapped the headphones back on and heaved the cart into the restroom. Chaz felt lost. Donovan had become a regular part of his night, and as he looked out over the empty store buzzing with vacuums, he was as lonely as he'd ever been.

He went down to the mailroom and turned on the lights. High on the top shelf, below the air return, sat a large white envelope. He climbed up on the counter and pulled it down; it was from GKD Systems and was addressed to Judy Luitweiler. He walked down the hall to the back entrance and pushed through the door. The Dumpster was at the far end of the loading dock. He ripped the envelope to shreds before tossing it up into the Dumpster. In the rush of the season, he knew that no one would be wondering where the results of those prints were. He slammed the Dumpster lid shut. Now he could collect his last paycheck without any problems, and no one would ever know.

SEVEN

Laughter is the shortest distance between two people.
—Victor Borge

Miriam turned the lights on in the kitchen at one thirty. She jumped when she saw me sitting at the table in the dark, my hands wrapped around a cup of tea. A red notebook sat opened on the table in front of me.

"I'm sorry, Miriam," I said. "Did I wake you?"

She squinted in the light and moved to a chair, sitting down. "I just seemed to jump awake and couldn't go back to sleep."

I swirled the last of the tea around in the cup and watched it slosh up and down the sides. "Another case of the jump-awakes," I said. "I jumped awake at twelve forty-two, the same time I always wake up on this day."

"Why is that?" she said.

I drank the last of the tea and stared at the empty bottom. "It's the time Walt died."

Miriam was quiet. "I lost Lynn at three oh-seven in the afternoon, and no matter what I'm doing on that day I just know what time it is and everything stops."

I nodded, cinching my robe tighter. "Lynn was a very kind man. He was good to you. I could tell."

She laughed. "He *was* a kind man. People loved Lynn. His students admired him and I adored him. He had a goodness in him that attracted people. Although we were a couple, everyone just naturally took to him over me. He was very affable with people. I've never been that way."

"I never noticed," I said.

She shook her head and smiled. "I can be an opinionated snob." I didn't say anything. "You know it's true, Gloria!"

"Well, I might have phrased it differently," I said.

She brushed her hand in the air. "However you phrase it, it's all the same. I've said things that I've regretted. I've let the door close on relationships and I've regretted it. Lynn never did that." She leaned back in the chair and crossed her arms. "What was your husband like?"

I looked up at the ceiling and sighed, smiling at the thought of him. "He was a tall and splendid man. I met Walt when I was eighteen years old. He was thirty-four and my mother begged me not to get involved with him, but he was so different from the boys in our small Georgia town. He had a mind and a soul that I just loved being around. We married and my mother thought I'd lost my mind. You know when I got married no one, not even my mother, explained the lifetime of commitment that it would take to make our marriage work. Nobody told me that during that first year or two you just kind of muddle your way through."

"Lynn and I managed to muddle through twenty-five years together," she said.

"Thirty-five for us."

"And how many children?"

I stood and walked into the dark living room, picking up an eight-by-ten photo from the mantel. I handed the family picture to Miriam. It had been taken when I was in my thirties and still had curves in the right places. Walt stood beside me, along with our three older children, and our toddler sat on my lap. "That's Andrew, our oldest. He was seventeen there. He has three children and is a computer programmer now." I pointed to our daughter with long, brown hair. "That's Stephanie. She lives just about ten minutes from here and has two children. She's a medical transcriber and is able to work at home. That's Daniel," I said, pointing to our son with reddish brown hair. "He was thirteen in that picture but now has two children and works for a land-development company in Georgia." I pointed to the toddler on my lap. "And that's Matthew, our youngest."

Miriam looked at him. "What does he do now?"

I shook my head, staring at his face. "I'm not sure."

"Is he married?"

"No one knows," I said, taking the picture and wiping the dust off with my sleeve. "He left home when he was seventeen, right before his father died, and we haven't seen him since."

Miriam was speechless. I could see the wheels turning in her head. All this time, and we knew so little about each other. "Why, Gloria?"

I poured another cup of hot water over a fresh tea bag and fetched a cup for Miriam. "So many reasons, I guess. He hated school and did poorly in it. Of course, we said he had to go to school and he hated it even more. Daniel also struggled through every subject, but he liked school and all my kids got involved in sports and music, but Matt was just so different. He could never find a place for himself at school, or anywhere else for that matter. If there was a rule he was set on breaking it, and if we told him he had to do something he did the opposite. Seems everything was an effort for him." I put the cup of tea in front of Miriam, along with cream and sugar. "For years after he left, I just kept replaying everything over and over in my mind, wondering what Walt and I had done wrong, what we should have done differently, because we made mistakes. I know we did." I reached for a napkin in the middle of the table and handed it to Miriam. "But I know I made so many more than Walt. When he got sick I focused all my energy on him; I was so involved with every breath, that I couldn't pay attention to . . ." I stopped. "I don't know. If I could go back. We always say that, don't we?"

Miriam rested her chin in her hand, shaking her head. "You can raise all your children in the same house, with the same rules, the same parents, the same patterns, but they all come away with a different outlook. My own two did. Gretchen calls all the time. Jerrod never has time. Gretchen is full of life. Jerrod can suck the life out of a room in a matter of minutes."

I propped my elbows up on the table, holding the cup. "I had a baby girl when Matthew was ten, and he was so excited, but we knew that Anna was very sick and the doctors didn't give us any hope. Every day Matt prayed for his sister and Walt and I tried to explain that sometimes people don't get well, but he never believed it. He never believed that God would allow a child to die. But she did, and something changed in him."

"Was he angry?"

"It wasn't anger but disappointment, I think. He was disappointed in God and in the rest of us. Matthew was never mouthy to us. He was quiet, which in a lot of ways was worse. When Walt got sick, Matt just turned everything inward. Couldn't take it. Walter was sick for only about six weeks. That's it. Matt ran off two weeks before Walt died. The thought of his father dying was just more than he could handle. I was a mess and Walt kept saying, 'He'll be back, Gloria. He'll come home. I'm praying that God won't let him rest until he comes home.'" I ran my hand back and forth over the notebook. "Even as he was dying, Walt was the strong one."

I opened the notebook. "This was Matthew's journal. I didn't even know he had been keeping a journal over the years, but there are pages and pages of his thoughts in here." I turned to a page and started reading. "Today some doctors told Dad that he's sick. He and Mom have been quiet all day." I flipped the page. "Dad is dying and nobody's doing anything about it. He and Mom went to some office today and made sure the will was in place and insurance was taken care of. In the meantime, while they're filling out paperwork, Dad keeps dying." I sipped some tea and cleared my throat, turning the page. "I'm watching Mom love Dad right now. She's curled up next to him on the couch and holding his hand." My throat tightened and a tear rolled down my cheek; I flicked it away with my finger. I took a moment, finding my voice. "Dad was in bed all day today. I watched Mom take care of him and she talked to him like it was just a regular day, but her face is sad. He reached for her hand and she sat on the edge of the bed looking at him. I think she's memorizing his face now." I covered my mouth and paused. Miriam sat in the silence, waiting. "I can't watch Dad die anymore. This shouldn't happen to him or Mom. He always had faith, but how is that helping him now? God doesn't care. I'm not even sure God knows what's happening down here. If he did he'd step in a lot more and help people." I closed the notebook, wiping my nose. "And that was his last entry."

"I'm so sorry, Gloria. I had no idea," she said. I used a napkin to wipe my face and wadded it up in my hand. "And you've had no word from him . . . ever?"

"Nothing. We don't know anything, but keep praying that something will get through to him."

"But what if your prayers aren't helping?" she asked.

I snapped my head up. "Of course they are!"

"But what if they aren't?"

"What if they *are*?"

Her voice was soft. "But Matthew hasn't come home."

"It has to be his choice," I said. "We're not God's pawns. We're free to do whatever we want." We were both quiet.

I disappeared into the living room and took an envelope from the branches of the Christmas tree, showing it to Miriam. "Twenty or so years ago we went to one of Andrew's basketball games. They were playing a team from some little town in Georgia, a real depressed area, and the boys on the team were playing in jeans and shorts and anything they could get their hands on. You could tell they just didn't believe in themselves and they played pitifully that night. At one time Walt said, 'I wish I could buy those boys some uniforms.' I didn't say anything but I figured out where I could buy some uniforms, and at Christmas I put an envelope in the branches of the tree for Walt. It was his Christmas present and it read, 'A gift of uniforms has been given to the Fighting Eagles in your name.' I even included a picture of the team wearing their brand-new uniforms. Every year Walt and I tried to outdo each other with those envelopes in the branches." I tapped the envelope in my palm. "This is the last one I put on the tree for him. It's a promise that I'd never stop looking for Matthew."

"Is that why you asked Erin to stay here? Is that why you rummage through bags of dirty clothes and clean filthy refrigerators?" I ran the envelope back and forth in my hand and felt tears rimming my eyes. She leaned onto the table, looking at me. "Gloria, do you blame yourself for his leaving?" I didn't answer.

I stared down at the aged envelope and ran my finger across it. "My father used to say, 'Find what breaks your heart and get busy.' Just thinking that Matthew was out on the street broke my heart, and every time I looked at street people I'd feel it all over again and knew I had to do something to help. I've always prayed that someone, somewhere would do the same for Matt."

"He has no idea you moved here?"

I crossed into the living room and placed the envelope back among the branches. "No," I said. "But our relatives are still in our old town. He could find me through them." I sat at the kitchen table and folded my hands under my chin. "I was so lonely in Georgia. All our kids were gone. My husband was gone, and it was that silence, that deafening silence of widowhood, that just about drove me crazy. Walt had a recliner, an ugly green plaid one that we'd had for years, and he sat in it for as long as he could. After he died I sat in that chair all the time, wanting to be close to him. I don't think I got out of it the first eight months after he died. But then Stephanie called and said she was having a baby, so I got out of it. Then I got out of it the next day and the next and I thought, 'What am I doing here?' I kept thinking that Matthew would just come waltzing through the door, but that wasn't going to happen and I knew it. So I either sold off or gave to the kids most of our things, hauled the recliner off to Goodwill, and moved up here to be close to my first grandchild. Life is stronger than death, and I knew I needed to kick death in the choppers and get back to living again. Grandchildren have a way of bringing us to our senses."

She picked up her cup and held it in front of her. "And you keep the porch light on for Matthew," she said. I nodded. "Well, don't I feel foolish?"

"You didn't know."

"I don't know anything, it seems. But if Lynn were still here he'd know. He always knew about people."

"You know now," I said.

"I have not been very kind, Gloria."

"I have not been very kind, either, and I'm sorry for that. I even told people that your British accent was as real as the color of your hair." She laughed and propped her elbows on the table. "It seems I can help a stranger in the street but I can't help the stranger beside me." I leaned back in my chair. "I took too much pride in my ability to read character." I stopped. "In my inability, I should say." I was anxious to change the subject. "Would you like to get married again?"

She reared her head back and laughed. "Oh my, no! Two husbands in one lifetime are enough. I do miss the companionship, though." She danced her fingers in front of her, as if conjuring up the plan of the century. "If there was a way to join two houses together, separate them with a long breezeway of some sort, I could live in my house and a man in his house and we could share meals and good conversation together." Her eyes lit up with the thought. "But after dinner he'd just trot off to his home and I'd stay in mine. Who wouldn't be up for that?"

"It's revolutionary!" I said.

She cupped her hands around the tea, staring into it. "If I could have had Lynn longer, that would have been wonderful. He was the secret to our marriage. If only I could have met him when I was twenty instead of thirty-five."

"How long did you say you were married?" I asked.

"Twenty-five years."

I thought for a moment, looking down at the table. "So you were a widow at sixty?"

"Yes." She bolted upright. "I mean no! I married Lynn when I was . . ." Her mind raced for the numbers. "I was twenty-two when I married him!" I rested my forehead in my hands but my shoulders began to shake. Miriam jabbed her finger into the table. "What is wrong with you, Gloria? Why are . . ." She threw her hands in the air. "Oh, just forget it. But I *refuse* to be a member of AARP!"

I smacked the table, laughing. "Don't you take advantage of Senior Citizens Day at Wilson's?"

"Never!" she said. "I don't even go downtown on Wednesdays because people look at me and automatically think I'm old. I'm not old."

I straightened my back, saluting her. "Neither am I. As a matter of fact, I never even feel old until I go out in public. Then it's all downhill from there."

Miriam cackled and doubled over, holding the table for support. "Have you ever looked at yourself upside down in a mirror?"

"What?" I'd never heard of such a thing. Miriam ran for the toaster and held it low. I bent over in the chair, focusing on my reflection, and screamed. "What is that?" Miriam lost her balance and stumbled into the wall, snorting. "I looked like an alien!" I rubbed my eyes, erasing the image from my mind. "I scared myself!"

She put the toaster down with a thud and her pink chiffon robe billowed around her as she moved about the kitchen, flailing her arms. "Nobody warns you about old age," she said. "It just creeps up on you and makes tracks across your face. It's terribly rude and inconsiderate. The next thing you know your body sags, your vision fails, and you wrench your back picking up a book!"

"I fell downtown a few days ago," I said. "I practically tackled a young man I thought was Matt and then my feet just went right out from underneath me. I was so flustered that I forgot to go into Wilson's, which was the reason I went downtown in the first place!" Miriam held her teacup to her mouth and laughed into it. "When I was young I always envisioned myself being fit and lean at this age in the middle of a race with runners half my age. Who was I kidding?"

She ran a napkin back and forth in front of her, thinking. "When I was younger and working so much in the theater I always thought that there would be roles for me. Really dynamic roles portraying strong, vibrant women in the prime of their lives. And those roles are out there," she said, looking up at me. "For younger actresses. When you hit a certain age you're no longer strong or dynamic, and forget about the prime of your life. You're waaayy past that and are relegated to play someone's grandmother or tottering old neighbor. And I think it stinks." She pounded the table with her fist. "Age is just a number!"

"Sixty and proud of it!" I said.

She looked at me, bewildered. "You mean I'm actually *older* than you?"

I squeezed her hand. "It can be our secret."

She sighed, scratching her head. "I was thirty-five when I married Lynn, and my mum was sixty-two. I remember looking at myself in the mirror in my dress and saying, 'I feel like a teenager.' And she looked at me and said, 'So do I, babe.'" She placed her hands under her chin. "I still feel like a teenager."

I smiled. "So do I, babe."

She jumped up and started pacing the floor of the kitchen. "I refuse to buy into the *old* mentality."

I stood at attention. "Don't sell that garbage around here because we ain't buying it!"

She held her fingers out one at a time and crossed each one off in front of me as she rattled through her list. "I will *not* go to those ridiculous 'over-the-hill' parties with their ghastly gifts, I will *always* pay full price for a movie ticket, and never—I mean *never*—will I go to a restaurant at four o'clock in the afternoon just to take advantage of an early bird special!"

I raised my hand and Miriam clasped it; our hands held together in victory.

Chaz sat on a bench in the middle of the square after work. The wind swirled around his ears and he let it sting his cheeks and mouth. This was what it was like for Mike, except a hundred times worse because he'd stay there all night. The wind lashed at his face and Chaz pulled up his scarf.

He couldn't take the cold anymore, so he walked a few blocks down to the bar. It was closing, but the bartender let him sit at the counter and drink a couple of beers while he shut down the place. The smell of stale cigarettes saturated the half-lit room. Glasses clinked together in the room behind the bar, followed by the whoosh of a restaurant dishwasher. The bartender turned up the radio in the back and sang along with it, popping his head out long enough to pour Chaz another beer and collect his money. He downed the rest of the beer and walked out the door.

The temperature had dropped since the time Chaz had gone into the bar, and he pulled the gray tuque tight over his head. A car drove around the town square and he wondered who would be out at this solitary hour. It seemed that no one but people like Mike and him were wandering about. The car pulled beside him and the passenger window rolled down. "You live in the Lexington Apartments, right?" He leaned over and saw an older woman behind the wheel.

"Yeah."

"I've seen you walk back and forth into town," she said. "I can drive you home."

She looked harmless and he was freezing. "Sure." He opened the door and slid inside. "I'm not used to seeing people out at this time."

Her laugh was ragged and tired. "I should have been home hours ago. I was visiting my daughter and her family, and was stuck on the highway for three hours while they cleaned up an accident, some sort of tanker truck." She threw a hand in the air. "What a mess."

She drove past the house glowing with Christmas lights, and Chaz pointed to it. "Do those lights drive you crazy in your place?"

She turned and looked at them. "Not really."

"Somebody said they've been up since last Christmas."

She pulled into the parking lot and snow crunched beneath the wheels. "Yeah, they have."

He shook his head. "Seems there's somebody like that in every neighborhood." He pointed to his building and she drove toward it.

"They put the lights up for their son last year," she said, pulling in front of the building. "He was overseas in the military and was coming home for a couple of weeks in November. They put up the lights, decorated the tree, and bought gifts for an early Christmas, but he never came. Missing in action. They keep them up, you know, hoping."

There was nothing to say that could follow that, so he thanked her for the ride and closed the door. He ran up the stairs to his apartment and noticed that the woman didn't park in front of one of the apartment buildings but drove across the street, pulling into the driveway of the home with the Christmas lights. He stood in the breezeway and watched as she waited for the garage door to open and then pulled in, the door closing behind her.

EIGHT

Life's most urgent question is:
What are you doing for others?
—Martin Luther King Jr.

I tried calling Carla's apartment throughout the morning. Donovan wasn't a bother, but I did have deliveries to make to some of my families and wondered when Carla would come for him. We made cookies to pass the time. Donovan sat on the kitchen counter and mixed the batter with great flourish.

"Maybe I can take cookies to Spaz," he said.

"Who's that?" I asked, turning the oven to preheat.

"He works with Mom and watches me. We play Spider-Man a lot. He'd love to eat these."

"Well, take some to him!"

Miriam walked through the front door and looked rumpled from a morning of watching workmen at her home. "Your hair's all mixed up," Donovan said.

"Thank you," she said, hanging her coat.

"It looks like a cat's been playing in it."

I stirred the batter and laughed. Miriam's coiffed look had certainly come undone since she moved in. I said it was because she was finally feeling at home and letting her guard down. She said it was because most of her products were covered with mold in the swamp that was once her bathroom. I offered to let her use my products but she said she didn't use retail, whatever that meant.

Miriam dipped her finger into the batter and put a dab on the end of Donovan's nose. "How long might this lad be staying with us?"

"His mother will be taking him home today," I said. "But I do need to run things to some folks and I need to pick up a few bags of hats and gloves at Wilson's. Would you like to stay here with Donovan or run the errands for me?"

Miriam clacked her tongue, thinking. She watched Donovan make a batter mess on the countertop and then wipe it on his pants. "I'll opt for the errands."

Miriam hadn't thought much about what I did throughout the day, but when she pulled into the driveway of Lila Hofstetter's place to drop off a bag of children's clothes she felt unsettled. Who was this woman and what was she supposed to say to her? Lila threw open the door and launched into a series of doctor appointment stories, each one longer and more meandering than the last. Miriam hung on to the storm door by her fingertips, letting it close farther after each story, but Lila rambled on. As it inched closed Miriam declined Lila's offer to come in for coffee and bolted for the car. "I should have stayed with the kid," Miriam said out loud, searching the map for the next street.

She took a box filled with plates, towels, and sheets to an elderly woman named Carol, who lived near the River Road housing development. Miriam sat slumped in her seat, certain the car would come under gunfire, hooligans pouring out from all sides around her. Her eyes scanned front, back, side to side, front, back, side to side. She snatched up her purse and threw it into the trunk, then slammed it shut. Carol answered her door and Miriam screamed as a small wiry dog named Bennie sprang past her. Carol squealed, imploring Miriam to bring him back. Miriam darted across the parking lot in chase, but the dog ran beneath a car and began to shake. Miriam bent over and made kissing noises in his direction. "Here, dog," she purred. "Come to Auntie Miriam." He lifted a paw and ran his tongue from top to bottom. "Oh, you insolent cur," she said, breathless. Miriam squatted and snapped her fingers. She sighed, watching him, then dug through her coat pocket, pulling out a stick of gum. "Lookie here!" Bennie sniffed the air and crawled toward her. She crept backward, holding the gum close to the ground, and snagged Bennie when he took the prize. She ran with the dog at arm's length, as if he were a bomb, and deposited him back inside Carol's door. Miriam declined Carol's offer for a cup of coffee and a bite of banana bread and ran back to the car. She looked at herself in the rearview mirror and groaned, fixing her hair. "This is crude and uncivil," she grumbled.

She hung her head out of the window on more than one occasion for directions. "Just like a dog," she said. Art Lender gave her a hug when she handed him a bag of work clothes and groceries, and she stumbled backward. She also declined his offer for something to drink, choosing to get behind the wheel with as few words exchanged as possible. He watched as she hurried to the car and hung his head out the door, shouting, "Thank you, Miss Mary!"

She spun on her heels. "Am," she said, yelling. "Miriam."

By early afternoon she was exhausted, but still needed to pick up the bags at Wilson's.

Chaz was called in to work two hours early. There were more and more customers every day, which meant longer hours for employees. He kicked the salt and slush off his shoes and held the door open for an older woman whom he considered to be attractive. She thanked him and made her way to Marshall Wilson at the jewelry counter. "Marshall, I'm here to pick up the hats and gloves for Gloria," Miriam said.

"She said you were coming and they're ready to go. Chaz!" Chaz stopped at the top of the stairs and turned toward Mr. Wilson. "We've set aside a few bags for Miss Glory in Customer Service. Would you help get those?"

Chaz watched as she walked toward him; she didn't act like the woman he had pictured in his mind at all. She looked kind of uppity. "Is Donovan at your house?" he asked, leading her to Customer Service.

She made a high-pitched sigh. "Yes! Do you know him?"

Chaz picked up the bags with Miss Glory's name on them. "He comes in a lot when his mom's working."

"He thinks I'm a nutter," she said. "This morning he told me that my hair looked like a cat had played in it."

He led her through the store. "That sounds like him."

"Are you new here?" she said.

He opened the front door for her. "Yeah."

"I think you'll love it." Chaz always hated it when people told him he'd love something. "This is a wonderful place to live. The longer I live here, the more I appreciate it." He loaded the bags in her trunk and closed the lid. "Thank you so much." She looked down at his name tag, "Chad." People always got his name wrong but it didn't matter.

He walked across the parking lot and noticed the pretty blonde he had seen in Wilson's driving out of the alley between the law office and the store. She didn't notice him on the sidewalk, but he stopped and watched as she drove past before clocking in for the day.

Dalton and Heddy loaded the Christmas care packages into the back of their SUV and I shut my trunk. Donovan, Erin, and Miriam loaded into my car and I coordinated again with Dalton about delivering to apartments and homes on our lists before meeting at the church that was located on the downtown square. When the temperature was thirty-five degrees or colder the church staff opened the church basement and spread out cots for the homeless to sleep on. They opened their doors at seven and I wanted to be ready. We pulled up a few minutes before seven and I handed a bag of packages to Erin and Donovan and waited for Miriam. "I'll just wait here," she said, leaning over the backseat, yelling.

I walked to the rear passenger door, holding a bag. "It's too cold to wait out here."

"Just leave the keys," she said. "I'll be fine."

"Come on! I need help carrying these bags."

She leaned farther over the seat. "Really, Gloria, I've been doing this all day and I'm not cut out for it."

I was losing patience. "Cut out for what?" I said. "Helping people?" Miriam didn't budge. "Move! I'm freezing out here." Miriam scurried out of the backseat and I handed her a bag. "The red packages are for women and the green ones for men." I noticed a woman sitting on a bench in the town square. "Oh, there's Janet. She won't come in till late tonight. She doesn't like to be around people. Take a package over to her and I'll meet you inside."

Miriam snapped her head up to see Janet. "I don't want to go over there and give something to a woman who doesn't like to be around people."

I closed the trunk. "Around lots of people. She'll do fine with you." I made a shooing motion with my hand and Miriam stood still, watching Janet. "Be sure you say Merry Christmas, too," I said, screaming over my shoulder.

Miriam growled and stepped into the road. Her foot plunged into a puddle resembling a dirty, gray Slurpee and she shook her head, moaning. "I hate helping people." She shook her foot off and walked across the street. Janet stood up and began walking through the square. Miriam hurried before Janet got away, calling out, "Yoo-hoo. Hello there," as she ran after her.

Janet turned and Miriam waved the package in the air. "For you." Janet took the box but didn't say anything. "Some things . . . from Gloria . . . I mean Miss Glory . . . for you." Miriam stopped, aware of how awkward she sounded. "And happy Christmas." Miriam looked up and saw Chaz watching her from the entrance of Wilson's. She shrugged her shoulders and heaved the bag onto her hip, heading for the church.

. . .

Carla awoke at seven that evening. She was sore and groaned as she sat on the edge of the bed, and tears filled her eyes. There was no way out. She couldn't call the police and report Thomas; if she did she ran the risk of DFS discovering he was abusive and putting Donovan into a foster home again. She just had to figure out a way to keep Donovan away from Thomas until she could think of a way to get rid of him once and for all. She stood up and the pain in her ribs took her breath away, making her fall back onto the bed.

She cracked open the bedroom door and listened to hear whether Thomas was in the apartment. She inched her way to the front door and made sure the dead bolt and the chain lock were both secured, and then stepped into the shower. Her mother's voice rang through her head. She had attracted losers her whole life. The only male who had been faithful and who really loved her was Donovan, and she was at risk of losing him.

At eight o'clock she opened the front door and ran into Thomas. He pulled her close to him and she screamed in pain.

"Get back inside," he said, gripping her arm.

She felt panic swell in her chest, but she ripped

her arm away. "I have to pick up Donovan and take him to another sitter before work."

"To hell with the kid," Thomas said. "He's fine." He'd been drinking; she tasted it when he pressed his mouth over hers and she winced as he held her.

She pushed away and stumbled to the parking lot.

At nine o'clock Chaz slipped into the security office and dialed information for the number of the state police in Kentucky, a state he picked at random just because Mike had a southern accent. He didn't know who to talk to, but thought someone might be able to go through missing person files or something to see if any of them were Mike. He was transferred twice, and then ended up with someone's voice mail. "It's stupid to call so late at night," he said out loud, and hung up the phone.

Donovan ran into the office and leaped for Chaz's neck. Carla stood in the doorway and Chaz waved. She slinked out the door and he opened his bag for Donovan to pick the sandwich he'd want to eat.

"Hey," Chaz said. "I met your friend Miss Glory today."

"I stayed at her house."

"I know. She seems nice."

"She is nice," Donovan said. "Mom said I need to know her address just in case I get lost or something, so I remembered 814 Maple and got two things of SweeTarts for it."

"That's probably a good idea," Chaz said.

"We made cookies and she gave me some to bring to you, but I ate 'em all."

"Thanks! She said you told her it looked like a cat played in her hair."

Donovan chomped down on the sandwich. "I didn't say that to her. I said that to the other lady."

"She thought you said it to her," Chaz said. "That's pretty funny, though."

Donovan laughed at himself, and bits of sandwich blew out of his mouth. Chaz jumped and pretended to be grossed out, which made Donovan laugh even harder. Chaz's night always seemed to go faster when Donovan was around.

Erin pushed my door open at midnight. "Gloria! I think my water just broke."

My feet hit the floor and Whiskers bolted out the door. "Get in the car!" I groped for the light and pulled a sweatshirt that was lying on the end of the bed over my nightshirt. "Get dressed first, then get in the car. I shouldn't have let you help deliver those packages. It was too much for you." I pulled a pair of sweatpants from a drawer, and paused when I realized they in no way matched my shirt. "Where're my keys?" I pulled on the sweatpants and dug through the pockets before screaming, "Your keys are in your purse, you idiot!" I ran into the hall and grabbed Erin's arm. "It's early."

"I know it's early," she said. "I'm sorry."

"I mean the baby. The baby's early." Miriam squinted up the stairs as I led Erin down. "She's having the baby. She's having the baby!" Miriam turned in circles and felt up and down her body. I waved my arm, yelling, "It's your gown! You're wearing your gown." I realized I was saying everything twice but couldn't think long enough to fix the problem. "Go get your robe. Put on your robe," I said as Miriam tore off down the hall.

Erin groaned and I screamed when she did. "Oh, it hurts!" she said.

"I'd tell you it was going to feel better, but I'd be lying." She groaned louder and I yelled over the top of her head. "Miriam!" Erin bent over, holding her belly, and I shouted louder. "Miriam!"

"Where are my green wellies?" Miriam said, running into the living room.

"Where are your what?" I asked, helping Erin into her boots.

"My wellies! My green wellies!" She was spinning, looking around her.

"Would you just talk like a normal person?" I screamed.

"My rubber boots," Miriam said. She hiked up her robe and pulled on the green rubber boots. "How could she be having the baby?" she said wild-eyed. "It's early."

"We've already been through all that," I said, putting Erin's coat on her.

"I can't go out in public like this," Miriam said. "It's not Halloween."

I held Erin's arm and ushered her through the front door. "Shut up, Miriam!"

"What did you say?"

"She said shut up," Erin said, taking the steps with her legs wide apart. Miriam cinched her robe tight and ran beside us. I opened the passenger-side door and Erin dipped down to get inside.

"Don't put her in the front," Miriam said, lifting Erin's arm.

"She's the one having the baby," I said, pushing her back down. "She deserves to be in front!" Erin sat and lifted her legs inside.

"What about the air bags?" Miriam said, waving her arms as if being struck in an accident.

I pulled Erin's arm. "Get in the back." We helped Erin into the backseat and I searched around for my keys. "Where are the keys?" Miriam twisted in all directions, searching the driveway. "Where'd they go? I just had them!"

Miriam turned and shrieked, "They're in your hand!"

I screamed when I saw them. "Oh, you idiot, Gloria!" I was clearly no good in a crisis.

Miriam ran to the passenger side. "Turn *left* out of the driveway, because Baxter is closed." I turned right and Miriam jumped. "What are you doing? I just told you to turn left."

"You never told me to turn left!" I spun the car around and Miriam toppled into me.

"I most certainly did," Miriam shouted. "Didn't I, Erin?"

Erin groaned and threw her head back against the seat. "I don't care! Drive faster!"

I pushed the pedal while groping for my seat belt. "Everybody buckle up!" I turned to look at Erin. "You need a seat belt."

"I can't," she said.

"Miriam! Buckle her seat belt."

Miriam unsnapped her belt and it whizzed back into place. She crawled over the back of the seat and reached for Erin's. "My robe is caught," she said. She yanked on her robe, trying to free it. I felt through the folds of fabric and Miriam smacked my hand away. "Are you some sort of masher?!"

"It's in the door!" I said, turning onto Post Avenue.

Miriam opened her door ajar, tugged on the robe, then closed the door again. She crawled over the back of the seat and wrapped Erin's seat belt around her, snapping it in. She locked her own belt into place and looked up in time to scream as I raced in front of a delivery truck when I turned onto Grand.

Miriam held her stomach. "I think I'm going to throw up."

"Be quiet, Miriam," I said, bearing down on the wheel. She crossed her arms in a huff.

I swung into the front entrance of the hospital and threw the car into park. We lifted Erin from the backseat and threw an arm over each of our shoulders, running for the door. "We're having a baby!" we shouted.

"She's having the baby," I said as a woman in scrubs ran toward us with a wheelchair.

The woman helped Erin into the chair. "And you're the grandmothers! Will you be joining her in Delivery?"

Our answer rang throughout the hall as the nurse wheeled Erin to the elevator. "No!"

"Yes!" Erin shouted over them as the doors closed in front of her.

I rummaged through my purse, pulling out the contents in massive handfuls. "What are you doing?" Miriam asked. I was annoyed, and continued to dig to the bottom, retrieving several battered cough drops, nasal spray, and some tattered coupons. "Is there a reason for such behavior?" Surely, I hadn't left what I was looking for at home. I would be so angry with myself if I'd done something so stupid. In desperation I emptied the entire purse onto the floor and poked through the pile.

"Ah ha!" I said, holding a piece of paper in the air.

. . .

At twelve thirty Chaz found Carla cleaning up around Santa's workshop. She looked worse than she had the previous night. "He's sleeping," Chaz said over the vacuum. She nodded but wouldn't turn off the vacuum. Whatever was bothering her, she planned to keep it to herself, so he walked away.

"Could Donovan go home with you tonight?"

He turned to look at her. "Why?"

"Because I'm sick," she said.

"What's wrong?"

She held up her hands in a stopping motion. "I'm too sick to care for him right now. I just need someone to watch him tonight. That's it." She waved him off and clicked the vacuum back on.

He grabbed her arm, turning off the vacuum. "Wait a second!" he said. "Do I just keep him all day tomorrow, or do you come and—"

"I'll pick him up tomorrow. I just need to keep him out of the apartment tonight." She seemed panicked, but her voice grew calm. "I don't want him to get sick. If I'm not feeling better tomorrow, I'll take him to Miss Glory's."

Chaz agreed to let Donovan stay, but couldn't imagine what he'd agreed to; he'd never even taken care of a cat before.

At the end of his shift, Chaz carried Donovan into his apartment and laid him down on the futon. He rubbed his eyes in the glow of the Christmas lights from across the street, and Chaz tried to turn his face away from the window. "Am I at your house?" Donovan asked.

"Yes," Chaz said, whispering.

"You don't have any furniture."

"I know." Chaz closed Donovan's eyes and Donovan flung an arm over his leg. Chaz tried to get up; he needed to get to the refrigerator.

"Lie down," Donovan said, half asleep.

Chaz moved Donovan's hand and pulled off his shoes. "I'll be right back."

"It's time for everybody to be asleep," Donovan said. "Even I know that." Chaz sat down on the futon, hoping Donovan would drift off again. Donovan put his hand in Chaz's and pulled it toward him. "Lie down and go to sleep." Chaz lay down next to Donovan and waited for him to fall asleep. Donovan put his hand on top of Chaz's chest and patted it. "I love you, Spaz."

Chaz didn't respond; he couldn't. When he was

confident that Donovan was asleep he moved his hand and slid off the futon, onto the floor, and buried his head in his hands. Tears fell into his palms, and he rubbed his coat sleeve over his face. He'd once heard his mother tell a friend that the drought was always worst right before the rain. He'd been living in droughtlike conditions for years because his life had dried up ages ago; there wasn't anything life-giving in him. He'd had so many plans and visions when he was a child, but they were gone now. When he'd dreamed as a boy, he never envisioned himself eking out a living and either losing or drinking away what money he made. He stopped planning and dreaming a long time ago because all he could see was the gaping wound of his life, which hit him square in the face day after day. Maybe that's what the truth does, it beats the living hell out of us until we do something about it. For years he shoved the truth aside, choosing to deal with the pain any way that he could, but he couldn't deal with it any longer.

Let it rain, he said into his hands. *Please let it rain.*

NINE

The black moment is the moment when the real
message of transformation is going to come.
At the darkest moment comes the light.
—Joseph Campbell

Carla knocked on my door but I wasn't home. She
waited in the driveway with Donovan, but after
an hour she pulled away and drove to her apartment.
Thomas's car was still there, so she backed away before he could see her. "What are you doing?" Donovan asked.

"Going back to wait at Miss Glory's," she said.
"You need to stay with her today."

"Why? I liked staying with Spaz."

She turned to him and her eyes blazed. "Don't
fight with me today."

· · ·

Miriam and I pressed our noses to the nursery window and smiled. Erin's mother, Lois, arrived an hour after I called. She was there for the birth of her first grandson and held Erin's hand throughout the delivery. Miriam and I bowed out of the room when Lois arrived and paced in the waiting room together, sipping bad coffee and watching horrible TV. When the doctor told us the news at eight o'clock that morning we cheered and hugged his neck as any grandmother would do, and fought to be the first to hold little Gabriel when we saw him with Erin. I won.

Donovan ran for the car when I pulled into the driveway. "Señorita Cuckoo!"

I wrapped my arms around him and looked at Carla. "What's wrong?" I asked.

Carla eyed Miriam and looked at the ground. Miriam took the hint and reached for Donovan's hand, leading him inside.

I stood with Carla in the driveway and searched her face. "Is he back?" Carla shook her head and wrapped the scarf tighter around her neck. "Are you lying?"

Her eyes were dark. "No."

"I don't believe you," I said. Time after time I'd seen battered women lie about being abused, with black-and-blue marks clearly on their faces.

Carla watched Donovan through the window and ran a finger under her nose. "He's not back, Miss Glory," she said. "I'm sick."

I turned Carla's face so I could look at her. "What's wrong? Do you need to go to the doctor?"

"I don't think so," she said. "It's the flu. You know. It works itself out." She folded her arms and shivered in the wind. "Miss Glory, could you please watch him for a couple of days till I feel better?"

I thought about it and Carla bit her lip, waiting. I felt uneasy, unsure of whether I believed her. "You're sure Thomas isn't there?"

She nodded. "I'm sure, Miss Glory. I haven't seen him."

"Will you go home and take care of yourself?" She nodded and I watched her slide behind the wheel and back out.

Carla didn't show up for work two nights in a row. Chaz asked Larry if she called him or anybody else on the janitorial team. "Haven't heard from her," Larry said. "She's probably snowed in like half the town." Twenty inches of snow had fallen in two days, and Mr. Wilson debated whether he should even open the store. Several employees couldn't make it in due to the weather, and Carla was probably just one of them. Chaz waited an hour and then went to the security office and dialed her number. There wasn't an answer. He tried again an hour later but she still didn't answer. A half hour later he let the phone ring for several minutes.

The store closed early due to snow, so Chaz finished his shift three hours earlier than usual. Larry drove him to his apartment. The streets were empty except for a plow that was trying to stay ahead of the snowfall, an impossible task by the looks of the snow that was piling on rooftops and cars. "Have a great Christmas," Larry said.

"You too."

"Do you work the day after?" he asked. Chaz nodded. "Better have somebody pick you up. You don't want to be out in this stuff."

Chaz closed the car door and stood in the parking lot, looking at his apartment. He could go in and drink till he fell asleep like one of the mannequin people his father talked about, or he could walk to Carla's to see if she was there. He ran up the stairs to his door and put the key in the lock. He'd never been good at interpreting that small voice inside; he never knew if it was just his mind thinking thoughts, or if there really was something in his soul nagging at him. The wind howled through the breezeway as he stood there, waiting, trying to figure it out. He reasoned that he could continue to call her apartment and rationalize later that he'd done all he could, or he could walk the three blocks to her place. "Damn it," he said, yanking the key out of the lock.

Carla's apartment was on the first floor; he saw a light in the window and hurried to get out of the cold. He knocked but she didn't answer; he knocked again and waited. The blinds were drawn on the window beside the door, so he peered through the cracks, looking for her or Donovan. Lights were on in the living room, and from what he could see it was a mess. He walked around the apartment and tried to see through the fence that surrounded the back patio. Snow had collected in between the slats of the wood, blocking his view; he jiggled the handle on the gate till the latch gave way.

The patio had the same view of the living room,

but the bedroom window was beside the patio doors.
He leaned over, straining to see inside. In the half-
light he saw Carla lying on her bed. He bent over the
patio rail and tried to rap on the window. He couldn't
get his arm to reach that far, however, so he picked up
a plastic baseball bat of Donovan's and whacked on
the window. She didn't move and he thumped on the
window again, harder this time. She still didn't move
and his heart rate jacked up. He rapped repeatedly on
the window, yelling her name. She lay still and he felt
his heart in his throat. He threw the small metal lawn
chair into the patio window but it bounced back to
him. The grill was small enough to handle so he
heaved it into the glass as he screamed for help. His
coat got in the way and he threw it off, then tried
again. The glass gave way a little. He slammed the grill
into the door two more times. He burst through the
hole he'd created and ran into Carla's room. A bottle of
vodka sat beside an opened bottle of prescription pills
on her bedside table. "What did you do?" he screamed,
feeling for her pulse. "What did you do?"

Paramedics loaded Carla into the back of the ambulance and one of them looked at Chaz, waiting. Chaz

jumped in and the paramedic slammed the door. Chaz sat where the EMT pointed and watched as they worked on Carla. It felt like the wind had been knocked out of him, and he bent over and hugged his knees. He needed to throw up, but couldn't. "Does she use?" The voice was loud in his ears. "Hey! Does she use?"

Chaz looked up. "No. I don't know."

At the hospital a flurry of people met the ambulance and chattered words to each other that Chaz couldn't follow. They rushed Carla into a room and a woman grabbed Chaz's arm, making him stay outside the door. After a few minutes—or an hour, for all he knew—a nurse with short brown hair and glasses on a chain around her neck flew through the door to his side. "You found her?" He nodded. "Are you a family member?"

"No. We work together," he said.

"Did she ever indicate that she was being harmed by anyone?"

"No. No, nothing like that."

"Her arm is broken," the nurse said. "She has cracked ribs and several bruises." She waited for him to say something. "Do you have any idea how those injuries happened?"

"No, I don't know anything about her personal life."

She went back inside the room and Chaz felt his hand start to shake. A middle-aged doctor with a high, round forehead and thin hair eventually came out and Chaz crossed his arms to stop the shaking.

"Vicodin and vodka," the doctor said. "Has she done that before?"

"I don't know," Chaz said.

The doctor nodded, looking him over. "Has she had any recent falls or been injured by anyone in a confrontation?"

"I told the nurse. I just work with her and she never told me anything about herself," Chaz said. "She didn't show up for work yesterday or today, and I live close by, so . . ."

"It's a good thing for her that you do."

"Is she okay? Can I see her?"

"She's currently unresponsive and will be going to ICU for further evaluation and care. We'll send someone for you before she goes."

He walked away and Chaz slunk into an orange, cafeteria-style chair down the hall. It felt like his body was oozing into the seat, and the shakes got worse. He leaned over onto his knees and heard footsteps in front of him, but it sounded like they were some-where in the distance. Electricity was surging through his body, making it quake. He rocked back and forth, trying to ditch the nausea, but it was still lodged in his throat. He looked up and down the hall and walked toward some doors at the other end. There were restrooms on either side of the hall, along with a storage closet and an employee lounge.

He ducked his head inside the lounge and saw that it was empty. His heart thumped in his ears but he opened one locker after another, looking for anything that would help. A noise outside the door sent him fleeing into the lounge's bathroom. He locked the door and flipped on the fan, waiting as someone opened a locker and rummaged through it. Perspiration settled on his forehead and back, and the shakes worsened. A bottle of mouthwash sat on the bathroom sink, and he grabbed it and twisted it open. He poured it into his mouth and drank till it was gone. The bottle fell to the floor and he leaned over the sink, dry-heaving. Sweat seeped through his hair and clung to his face, but after a few moments the shakes stopped.

He looked in the mirror and the sight he saw re-pulsed him. A few moments earlier he had looked at people who had broken bones or were bleeding in the emergency room, and he was raiding lockers to get a fix.

A knock at the door exploded in his ears.

"You okay in there?"

His heart raced faster at the sound of someone's voice, and he flushed the toilet. "Yeah. Sure," Chaz said. He turned on the water and splashed his face, then ran wet fingertips through his hair. He pulled out several paper towels and dried his face and hands, then opened the door. A man wearing a white jacket stood in the lounge. "I'm sorry. I was sick, but the stalls were full in the men's bathroom."

"Not a problem," the doctor said. "Do you need to see someone?"

Chaz threw the paper towels away and headed for the door. "No. I brought in a friend, and the whole thing just made me . . ."

"It happens." Chaz's back was to the doctor, but he felt him watching him. "Why don't you sit for a second? Nobody's in here but me."

"No, no," Chaz said, turning toward him. "I'm really sorry I burst in here. I'll get back down the hall."

The doctor touched his arm and looked at him. "Why don't you sit down?" Chaz sat in a chair covered with pastel flowers. The doctor sat opposite him and took his pulse. "I'm Nathan Andrews. I work upstairs in Pediatrics, but I'm still qualified to take the pulse of an adult." Nathan lifted one of Chaz's eyelids and Chaz closed his mouth tight, holding his breath.

Nathan crossed his arms and looked him over. "What happened to your friend?"

Chaz rubbed his hands up and down his jeans; his palms were sweating. "They think somebody beat her up."

Nathan made a grunting sound and shook his head. "You found her?" Chaz nodded. "She's fortunate that you did. You're a good friend." The words struck Chaz and he looked up at him. He couldn't remember the last time he'd been a good friend to anybody. "Are you going home for Christmas?" Nathan asked.

"No."

Nathan sat back, folding his arms. "Where is home?"

"I don't even know anymore."

"Why is that?"

"Just alone, that's all," Chaz said. "My parents are deceased."

"My mother died when I was little," Nathan said.

"No matter how old I get, I still miss her at Christmas. I look at the parents of friends of mine and think, 'My mom would be their age now.'"

Chaz nodded, shifting in his chair. "I do the same thing."

"What kind of work do you do?" Nathan asked.

"I, uh . . . nothing really," Chaz said. "I've had a lot of jobs. Right now I work in security."

"Great."

"When I was a kid I wanted to be a doctor."

Nathan crossed an ankle over his knee and leaned on it. "What happened?"

"I came down with a bad case of the stupids," Chaz said.

Nathan laughed and stood, walking to the door. "You're still young, though."

Chaz shook his head. "Nah. Not cut out for it."

"That's what I thought, too," Nathan said. "But it's never too late and you never know what's around the bend." He clapped Chaz on the back and made his way upstairs.

Chaz walked down the hall and fell into the orange chair again. He leaned onto his knees and pressed his fists into his forehead. He jumped when the nurse called him.

She let him sit beside Carla's bed, and pulled the curtain between her and another patient, an older man who was hooked up to an IV. Carla opened her eyes when she heard him. "You look like hell," she said.

"So do you," he said as he stepped close to the bed. "Carla, you don't have to tell me anything, but . . . what were you doing?" A tear rolled down her face and she let it fall onto the sheets. "Were you trying to . . ."

She rolled her head back and forth. "No. No," she said. "I needed medicine to stop the pain, but it didn't help, so I took a few more, but they didn't work, so I kept on taking more."

"You should have called somebody," he said, stepping closer.

She shook her head, clenching the sheet in her hands. "No, I couldn't. I couldn't call anybody."

He sat down and looked at her. "There are people who care, Carla." She looked up at the ceiling. She didn't believe that any more than he would have; once you've convinced yourself it isn't true it's impossible to think anything else.

"They say somebody beat you up," Chaz said.

Another tear fell onto the bed. "Thomas." She lifted the sheet and wiped her face.

"You could have died," Chaz said. She nodded, and more tears spilled down her cheeks. "Donovan would have been alone just like that."

"He's better off alone," she said.

He leaned close to her. "No. He's not. Don't *ever* believe that. Nobody's better off alone."

A nurse ushered Chaz out of Carla's room before he had a chance to ask her if Donovan was still with Miss Glory. He walked out the front doors of the hospital and the cold air stabbed his lungs. His coat was still at Carla's but he pulled the hood of the sweatshirt over his head. He wandered through the hospital parking lot into the street and started to run. He stopped after two blocks and tried to catch his breath; it was too cold to run. He had to find Donovan; he needed to see him. *Help me find him. Help me find Miss Glory's home.* He hadn't prayed in years, and he felt foolish.

The bartender from a few nights before saw Chaz as he was driving home and gave him a lift to Wilson's. From there he ran through the town square over to Baxter, then behind the homes on that street to Maple.

What was the address Donovan had rattled off? He

thought hard but he couldn't hear the number in his
head. It was something 14. 214? 514? His hands
ached and he shoved them deep inside the sweatshirt
pockets, pressing them close to his stomach. The
frozen asphalt seeped through his tennis shoes and
he realized his toes were numb. What was he doing?
He ran farther still and saw a porch light on in the distance. Snow sat on top of each mailbox like a frosty
top hat, and he swiped it away from the top of one:
860. Snot drained out of his nose and onto his hand;
he hadn't even felt it. He wiped it away with his
sleeve and his nose stung at the touch. He walked farther and knocked snow from another mailbox: 832.
Was the house number 814? He thought it was, and
tried to speed up but couldn't. He put his head down
in the direction of the snow and counted the steps he
took. What if no one answered the door? What if they
called the police? The air burned his lungs and he
buried his nose in his sweatshirt. He flicked snow
from another mailbox and held on to his side as he
read the number: 820. It hurt to take deep breaths, so
he took shallow ones instead, counting the number
of houses down to 814. It was the one with the porch
light on. He pulled his sweatshirt up over his nose
again and headed toward it. The street was empty and

all the lights were off inside the house. It was two o'clock in the morning. He stood at the bottom of the driveway and hated himself for coming all this way, but the image of Carla lying on her bed jumped into his mind and he had to know that Donovan was safe. Even though the doorbell was lit he chose to knock on the door instead, hoping not to wake everyone in the house. He knocked again and heard footsteps.

"Who's there?"

"Miss Glory, I gave you the bags filled with hats and gloves at Wilson's the other day," he said, shivering.

The dead bolt clicked and the face of the woman that he knew as Miss Glory appeared in the opening. "What are you doing?"

"I'm really sorry," he said. "Something's happened to Carla and I just needed to know if Donovan was here."

"Yes he is, but . . ."

"What's wrong? Who is it?" Chaz heard another woman's voice. She came and stood beside Miss Glory inside the darkened entry.

The chain lock fell, the door widened, and the second woman screamed the loudest, most hair-raising scream he'd ever heard.

TEN

A mother's yearning feels the presence of the
cherished child even in the degraded man.
—George Eliot

His hands were shoved inside his pockets just as I
remembered seeing him as a child waiting for
the school bus. His face was thinner and masked with
stubble, but his father's brown eyes peered out beneath the hood of the sweatshirt. I reached for him,
trembling as I pulled him inside. "Matthew, my
Matthew," I said over and over, holding his arms so
my knees wouldn't buckle. "It's you. It's you."

"Mom." His voice was so small that I barely heard
him. He cried as he held on to me and I wrapped my
arms around him, weeping.

"It's you, it's you, it's you," I said, burying my face
in his. I cupped my hands on his face and searched
his eyes. "You're home," I said, my voice failing me.

"You're home." I led him to the sofa. "Miriam, bring blankets." She ran from the darkened room in slow motion but was back in an instant, and wrapped blankets around his shoulders.

Miriam flipped on a lamp beside Matthew; tears were on her face but she didn't say anything. She helped take off his tennis shoes and socks, then wrapped his feet in a blanket. She draped blankets over his legs and then backed away and fell into a chair. I sat beside him, not fully comprehending what was happening, and touched Matt's cheek to make sure he was real. "Every day I saw your face." I choked on the words. "Every single day I prayed and prayed that you would come home." My throat tightened and I squeaked out the words "my son, my baby."

I threw my arms around his neck and we sobbed as we held each other. There was nothing pretty about it. There are no words to describe how much I had missed my son and the sound of his voice. Words were lodged somewhere in my mind but I couldn't form them in my mouth. I just kept saying "I love you" over and over again. After years of hiding, my child was finally home.

. . .

When the haze started to settle Matthew began to shake and I clutched his hands to warm them. Miriam brought him a cup of hot coffee but it sloshed over the cup's rim when he took it. He was embarrassed and ran his hands through his hair; they trembled as he rubbed his face.

"Miriam, there's a bottle of wine above the stove. Could you bring that in so we can celebrate?"

"What you cook with? You want . . ."

"Above the stove," I said, over her. "Please." Miriam poured what wine was in the bottle into a glass and handed it to Matt. She looked at the bottle and then at me. There wasn't enough to go around. She poured a small amount into the bottom of my glass and I cocked my head toward Matt. She glanced at me and then filled his glass again.

Matthew wouldn't face me; he kept his head down, holding the empty glass between his knees. "After seven years this is all I have to give you, Mom." He began to cry and I leaned over, wrapping my arms around him.

I put my hand on his face and looked into the brown eyes I had seen in my mind every day for the last seven years. "You are your father's son. You look just like him."

He shook his head. "I'm not the son you remember." He leaned onto his knees. "I'm nothing like Dad."

It was the first time he'd really grieved for his father, and huge tears streamed down onto his hands. Years of running and hiding and disgrace washed over him. "I'm sorry, Mom." His voice was high-pitched and strained. "I hurt you and Dad so much. I thought it would be better somewhere else, but it never was." Miriam tried to excuse herself more than once but I motioned for her to sit down. There were no secrets as far as I was concerned.

I called Dalton and Heddy as soon as I learned about Carla. Dalton was asleep and I found myself shouting into the phone to make him understand. I didn't tell them everything, but I let them know that someone ended up at my house who had found Carla. They were going to go to the hospital to be with her right away.

In the early morning hours I learned that Matthew had been living just an hour north for the last two years. "You were so close," I said over and over again. "So, so close." When I discovered he'd moved here just three weeks earlier to take the job at Wilson's I threw my hands on top of my head.

"I thought you were Miss Glory when you came to the store a few nights ago," Matthew said, looking at Miriam.

She tossed her head back and laughed. "Oh my, no! Your mother is the only Miss Glory around here." He looked at me, confused; there was so much to talk about. "But your name was Chad or something, wasn't it?" Miriam asked.

He looked at me. "Chaz. I went by Chaz."

"Your dad's middle name?"

He nodded. "Chaz McConnell."

My maiden name. Although he had been hiding, Matthew managed to keep a part of his family with him. He couldn't leave everything behind.

I showed him to Erin's room just before sunrise. By the looks of him I thought he'd sleep for days. I felt like I would, too.

"Our other roommate normally sleeps here," I said, tossing some of her things into the closet. "But she just had a baby and is with her mom." I pulled the shade down and kissed him on the cheek. "It's finally Christmas," I said, squeezing his hand. It was the first time he'd stood in front of me in the light and I noticed his shoulders, hands, and chest. They were no longer underdeveloped as I remembered. His face had lost the baby fat he used to have and was now covered in stubble; his cheekbones stood out full and strong. It was a man's face. His father's eyes looked at me but they didn't light up the way Walt's did, and it broke my heart.

"So many times," he said. He ran his hand over his chin and looked around the room. "I wanted to come home . . . but couldn't." He shuffled his feet and stared at the floor. "I've done so many things . . ." His eyes glistened and he glanced up at the ceiling, clearing his throat. "I just couldn't come back then. I couldn't do that to you."

I grabbed both of his hands. "You could always have come home. No matter what you had done."

He shook his head. "No. I couldn't." Shame is a bully; it likes to hang around, tapping us on the shoulder from time to time; then it pounds us in the face. Matthew had taken a lot of poundings over the years.

I put my hand on the side of his face. "You've always been my son. Nothing could ever change that." I sat on the end of the bed with him. "After you left and your father died I couldn't wait for some days to be over. I was so lonely and so angry that I'd rant and rave and finally say, 'I need a new day right now.' And another day *would* come and I'd manage to get through it." I held his hand. "There was always enough mercy to manage." I turned his face to look at me. "There is *always* enough mercy to manage." I kissed his forehead. "You're home. *You are home*," I said, whispering in his ear. He nodded and I prayed that he'd believe it.

"Get some sleep," I said, and closed the door behind me. The banister held me up as I crept downstairs. In my heart I knew what my son had become and felt sick to my stomach.

Miriam met me in the kitchen. "I was present at a miracle," she said, handing me a cup of coffee. I sat at the table and felt my muscles turn to butter; every bone and ligament went soft. "It was a miracle, wasn't it, Gloria?"

"I don't know," I said, finding my voice. "If it was a miracle, why am I so scared?"

She knelt in front of me, keeping her voice low. "Because miracles make our knees buckle and our palms sweat. They leave our heads spinning and our hearts racing. If miracles didn't make us feel like jumping up and down one second and vomiting the next, then it'd be just another day." She stopped and smiled. "And this was not just another day, Gloria."

Stephanie was out of state with her family visiting her husband's brother when I called the next morning. From her brother-in-law's phone she was able to conference in my other two sons. I was hoarse and exhausted after I finished talking with them.

Heddy screamed when I called her. She dropped the phone and ran to get Dalton. I heard her hollering through the house, followed by muffled dialogue as she described details of the night to Dalton. "Hello," I said, yelling into the phone. More conversation followed and Heddy got louder the longer she talked. "Hello!" I screamed. She made me laugh as I listened, pressing the earpiece close to my ear.

The phone rattled and thumped on the other end before Heddy picked it up again, breathless. "Hello? Gloria?" She heard me laughing and I could envision her slapping her head.

We talked about Carla and her situation and decided that it wouldn't be enough if she just changed the locks on her apartment doors. If Thomas wanted in he'd figure out a way to get past the locks. Heddy suggested that Carla and Donovan stay with them until Carla could find another place to live. Donovan would stay with them until Carla got out of the hospital.

They picked Donovan up thirty minutes later, after he'd eaten breakfast. He wanted to get home as fast as he could to check on the Christmas bush. After three days without water he was certain the bush must be close to death. "Santa won't put presents under a dead Christmas bush," he repeated throughout the meal.

As I bundled him up to go, I kissed his face. "Thank you, Donovan."

He wiped away the kiss. "What for?"

There wasn't enough time in the day to help him understand. He had slept through Matt's arrival, camped out, as usual, in my room in a makeshift tent of quilts and blankets. I kissed him again and hugged him close before lying down on the sofa to sleep. If Matthew came down the stairs I wanted to hear him. Images from the night reeled through my mind and I smiled.

Miriam was right. A miracle *had* taken place, and we had all played our parts in it.

. . .

When I awakened I felt terrible and wondered if I would have been better off not sleeping at all. I opened the curtains in the kitchen. Through the window I saw Miriam at her house, surveying the work the men were doing there. I hadn't heard her walk past me and wondered if Matthew had left also. His shoes sat by the door, however, so I crept upstairs to shower. I put on my navy blue jersey knit pants with a white turtleneck and a matching blue jacket before running a pick through my curls. I pinned back the unruly ones and put on some makeup. I stared at myself in the mirror. "The barn sure needs more paint today." The brush flew across my cheeks. I was reaching for my Morning Rose lipstick when the doorbell rang. I ran the tube over my bottom lip and looked at myself, shrugging. "It's the best I can do." The doorbell rang again and I ran down the stairs, tripping over the cat. "Move it, Whiskers!"

Erin held the baby on the porch and her mother, Lois, stood behind her with a diaper bag. I took Gabe and led them inside, then told them what happened, blabbing as fast as I could. "Long story short—Matthew is sleeping in your room right now!" Erin fell onto the recliner and her mother gaped at me, searching for words.

"He's here?" Erin asked. "He's actually in this home?"

"He's home." I kissed Gabe and looked down at his face. "Babies are being born and children are coming home. Now that's what I call Christmas!"

"I was going to pick up some of my things," Erin said. "But I'll come back another time."

"No, stay. You can meet him."

"This is your time," Lois said. "We'll come back."

"Are you going back to Layton and Associates?" I asked.

Erin threw the diaper bag over her shoulder. "I'll go back on Tuesday. Jodi said they'll be needing someone full-time soon, and I don't want to miss my chance at it." She ran her finger over Gabe's nose. "It's a new chapter, you know?"

It seemed we were all learning about new beginnings and starting over.

After years of working with folks in this town, I've discovered that people want to change when what they've been doing doesn't work for them anymore. Call it what you will—an epiphany, an awakening, or a stirring of the soul—whatever it is it raises you to your feet, maybe for the first time in your life, and you are determined that this time you will change. That's why Matthew called AA—not because I told him to, but because his life wasn't working for him anymore. His head pounded and his tongue stuck to the roof of his mouth as he looked up the phone number in the yellow pages late that morning. Sometimes when you want a new life, you want it to start as soon as possible.

On Monday morning he drank half a carton of orange juice to help his dry mouth, and stood for ten minutes in the shower at his apartment before popping a couple of Xanax pills. He walked to the AA meeting at the church alone—it's how he wanted to do it. The smell of cigarette smoke filtered up onto the street from the stairs that led to the basement. People lined the steps, taking one final puff before entering. Matt made his way through the smoke and the steel door clanged shut behind him as he walked down the darkened hallway to an open door. A table with coffee was set up at the front of the room. He poured himself a cup.

"You new?" Matt turned and saw a man dressed in khakis and a turtleneck sweater looking at him.

"Yeah."

"Good to have you," the guy said, as he stirred cream into his coffee.

Smoke clung to the drapes, and the carpet bore coffee stains from the members' presence in the building. "What in the world do the people upstairs think of this?" Matt said.

The guy shrugged. "They think enough of it to let us come back each week." A man started to talk behind them and the guy in the turtleneck motioned for Matt to sit. The room was set up in two semicircle rows of metal chairs. Matthew sat in the second row, behind a post and next to the cumbersome air ducts, hoping no one would notice him. He slunk down and studied what lay beneath his fingernails.

The room hummed with chatter as it filled to over fifty people. There were mechanics and bank presidents, beauticians and corporate trainers. They wore suits, flannel, scrubs, silk, khakis, and blue jeans, and ranged in age from teenagers to a seventy-seven-year-old man. They were a diverse bunch. By all appearances they had nothing in common save one thing. They wanted a new way to live.

A gruff man in a denim shirt and jeans brought the meeting to order. "My name's Lukas and I'm an alcoholic." Everyone greeted him, and Matt leaned over on his knees, feeling awkward and obvious and embarrassed to be there. An older man walked in late and sat next to him, but Matthew didn't look at him. Lukas read about community from the AA Big Book. He opened the floor for discussion, and within seconds the room was buzzing.

A man named Coley took the floor. "When I look back, I know that I'm capable of repeating anything I've ever done, and that scares me to death," he said. A few members nodded and Matthew leaned over in his seat to hear Coley over the heating system. "For the longest time I thought life had to be lived up here where everything is exciting and you do what you want, when you want. But as much as I tried that I'd end up down here, just scraping along. Now I know that life's good right here in the middle." He smiled and threw his hand in the air, indicating that he was done.

The conversation ricocheted from person to person for thirty minutes without a break, when the man next to Matthew cleared his throat.

"Hello, Frank," the members said when he introduced himself.

"I've been sober for twenty years this month," Frank said. The room erupted in applause. "When I first started coming to these meetings a man spoke up and said, 'We're as sick as the secrets we keep.'" Matthew turned to look at him. "My addiction was private, and as a man I wanted to be able to fix myself in private but I couldn't. Pain's a great motivator. We weren't meant to be isolated. We need each other. That's why I come here."

Around it went for another twenty minutes before Lukas took control again and somebody gave out "sobriety chips." Tim got a thirty-day chip, and Frank received one for twenty years. When the meeting ended, Matthew avoided the other people and raced up the stairs to the street. It was snowing again, and he pulled the hood of his sweatshirt over his head and zipped his coat up to his neck. Words from the meeting flew through his mind. *I brought on a lot of chaos in my life,* Tim had said. *I hated what I had become,* a woman in her fifties had said. A dusting of snow blew across the sidewalk and Matthew walked faster. He heard a truck, and turned when it slowed down next to him. It was Frank.

"Need a lift?"

"I'm headed to the Lexington Apartments," Matt said.

"I go right by there," Frank said, stopping. Matt

slid in and closed the door. "I'm Frank," he said, extending his hand. "First meeting?" Matthew nodded. "The steps work if you work them."

Matthew stared out the window. "What if you can't get through them?"

"Then they don't work."

"It's not easy, is it?" Matt said.

"Adult problems are never easy," Frank said. "Seems someone along the way should tell us that. Have a little graduation ceremony or something."

"What if I'm not sure if I really have a problem?"

"Anybody suggest you come to this meeting?" Matt shook his head. "Anybody *force* you to come? Court ordered?" Matthew looked at him. "You came on your own?" Matt nodded and watched out the window as Fred Clauson spread salt on the sidewalk in front of Wilson's. "Then you're sure you have a problem." Matt liked Frank. He was blunt but kind.

"It seemed pretty raw back there," Matt said.

"They're the most honest people you'll ever be around," Frank said. He looked over at Matt. "So why'd you come?"

"I left home when I was seventeen, right before my father died," Matt said. "Drinking helped . . ."

"Numb the shame?"

Matthew nodded. "For months I haven't been able to put a thought together in my head. I was losing ground every time I turned around, but I couldn't stop—I couldn't stop anything I was doing. I found my mother and thought . . ." His eyes filled with tears and he turned away.

"This is it?" Frank asked. Matt nodded. Frank pulled into the apartment parking lot, stopped the truck, and looked at him. "You want to come back?"

"Sure, but I've never finished anything in my life."

Frank laughed. "Then you'll fit right in!" He folded his hands over the steering wheel and leaned into it. "Here's the nuts and bolts: Don't go in your apartment and think that you'll never take a drink again. You will. But when you do, don't let it keep you pinned to the floor." Matt nodded. "What are you popping in the morning to help you get up and out?"

"Xanax."

"Don't convince yourself you'll be stopping those cold turkey, either. You want a sponsor?"

"I don't know what one does."

Frank wrote down his phone number. "I won't call you, but you can call me anytime, day or night. Call me when you want to take a drink. Call me when you wanted to take a drink but didn't. Call when you did drink and you hate yourself for it afterward. Call me if you're happy, sad, excited, or mad as hell. That's what a sponsor does. See you tomorrow?"

Matt got out of the truck. "Sure."

"Call me if you want a ride."

Frank waved and Matthew watched him pull out of the driveway to the home across the street. He stopped at the end of his driveway and fixed the Christmas lights that were drooping on the baby pine tree. "You're kidding me," Matt said beneath his breath, watching as Frank went from tree to tree, shaking snow from each light strand. Matthew laughed and ran up the stairs to his apartment.

ELEVEN

If the will to walk is really present,
God is pleased even with your stumbles.
—C. S. Lewis

Matt cut across the town square on his way to work Tuesday afternoon and noticed the pretty blonde driving through town. She pulled into the alley that went behind the law office. He ran past the gazebo and fir trees to the street, then waited for cars to pass and dodged one as he ran into the road, crossing over to Wilson's. Her steps were brisk as she hurried up the alley; she didn't see him dart in front of the law office.

"Hi, I'm Robert. Can I help you with something?"

Robert's voice startled Matt and he stepped away from the entrance, shaking his head, then opened the door for Robert. Matt turned in a snap to wait for the blonde and accidentally knocked a stack of files out of her hands. "I'm sorry!" he said. "I opened the door for a guy and had no idea you were . . ." He helped pick up the scattered files and handed them to her. She smiled and looked lovely. In the pit of his stomach he knew it wouldn't work. She was beyond him.

The phone was pressed to Judy's ear. "Is Mr. Wilson in?" Matt asked, whispering. She motioned for him to step up to the office behind her.

Marshall was at his desk, making notes on a legal pad. "Hello, Chaz. What's up?" He took off his glasses and leaned back in his chair.

Matt stood motionless by the door and fumbled with the gloves in his hands. "My name's not Chaz McConnell."

Mr. Wilson sat on the edge of his desk and pulled off his glasses. "I don't think I'm following you."

Matt shoved the gloves into the pockets of his coat. "I bought a Social Security number from a guy a few years ago because I couldn't use mine," he said. Marshall rubbed his brow, trying to understand. "I've never had to be fingerprinted before and I was afraid that the person with the Social I bought would have a criminal record. I also knew that my fingerprints wouldn't match the number, and once someone found out I'd get fired. So I threw the envelope away when it came in."

Marshall nodded, thinking. "Why didn't you want to use your own Social?"

"Because I ran away from home seven years ago," Matt said. "I never wanted my family to find me. I just found them on Sunday night, though. My mother's Gloria Bailey."

Marshall's eyes widened and he ran his index finger back and forth over his chin. "Well, Chaz." He looked up at him. "Or . . . ?"

"It's Matthew. My parents always called me Matt."

"All right, Matt. See Judy about taking a fingerprint test for the job. The security office is down the stairs at the end of the hall." He slid the glasses over his ears and sat down at the desk. "We're glad to have you." He grinned and never brought up the issue again.

Carla went to work early and ran down the stairs to the security office. She opened the door and watched

Matt for the longest time. He was uncomfortable and shifted in the chair. "What are you doing?" he asked.

She sat on the edge of his desk and crossed her arms. "Just trying to see Miss Glory in you."

He pushed away from the desk, setting his ankle on top of his knee. "You won't see much of her in me."

"She's in you," she said. "Donovan told me." She picked up a half-eaten candy bar and took a bite.

"How is Donovan?"

"He's tearing up Dalton and Heddy's house and thinks he's all that. I found a new apartment, though, so we'll move this weekend." She took another bite of the candy bar, thinking. "I never said thank you."

"You don't have to," he said.

"If you hadn't showed up, I don't know . . ."

"Don't think about it," Matt said.

She fidgeted with the candy wrapper. "I keep trying to piece things together. Donovan, your mom, this job. I still can't figure it out."

"Maybe you're not supposed to. Maybe that's the point." He picked up pens and pencils that were scattered across the desk and placed them in the cup that was sitting on the desk's edge.

"You sound like your mom." She reached for a

notepad and let the pages flap over her thumb. "You know, when I first met you I didn't like you."

He threw his arms in the air. "What? Why not?"

"I thought you were an—"

He put a hand up. "I know. Donovan told me."

She laughed and waved the notepad up and down in front of her. "Your mom makes me think about stuff. She tells me to eat green things and to make Donovan eat them, too. She tries to teach me how to make a budget and buy groceries and she tells me not to curse in front of Donovan and warns me about men. I haven't listened to that last part." He smiled and leaned back in the chair, propping his feet on the desk. "She makes me believe that I'm not a lost cause, you know?"

He nodded. "I hope to be like her when I grow up."

She got off the desk. "Good luck with that." She opened the door and Matt threw his feet to the floor.

"Hey, wait a minute!" he said. "You didn't say if you liked me now."

"Ask Donovan," she said, letting the door close behind her.

. . .

I stood in front of the Christmas tree and looked out onto the porch. "What are you doing, Gloria?"

Her voice startled me and I turned to see Miriam standing in the hall entryway. "I'm wondering if I should turn off the porch light."

She crossed through the dark room and sat down on the sofa. "Leave it on."

I looked at her in the half-light. "Really?"

"Shouldn't others see it?" she asked. "Lost ones looking for the light?"

I sat on the recliner, smacking my hands on top of my knees. "Miriam, that might possibly be the most profound thing you've ever said!"

"Nonsense," she said. "I'm full of insight and astute observations. Wisdom seeps through my pores." She leaned forward and the lights of the tree lit up her face. "Have you wondered, Gloria, if there's a reason . . . for all the pain?"

I rested my head on the back of the recliner. Whiskers jumped into my lap and I rubbed behind his ears. "I can't wrap my mind around it," I said. "But I'm sure there's a purpose."

She curled her legs up on the sofa. "Even if it's self-inflicted?"

Whiskers stretched a front paw toward my face

and I squeezed it in my hand. "If that's not the case then there's no hope for any of us."

She stood up and her gown and robe cascaded off the couch in smooth pink folds. "Good night, Gloria. Good night, cat."

I watched her disappear down the hall and heard the bedroom door close. For the rest of my life I could question why Matthew ran away, why he was gone for so long, and why he chose to do things that hurt him. I could ask myself things like, *What if Matt hadn't moved to this town? What if he hadn't just stumbled onto my doorstep? Would he ever have come home?* I knew I could play the "what if?" game forever. Or I could let God work beauty out of the last seven years and actually sleep at night. Whiskers jumped off my lap and I unplugged the tree, letting the porch light filter through the living room as I walked up the stairs to bed.

Matt took the bus into the city the next morning and walked four blocks to the Kirk shelter. A woman behind a semicircular desk led him through the gymnasium and wide double doors to a hallway with several doors on either side. The floors were shiny and smelled of ammonia and the walls were sage green.

She opened a door to a cinder-block room, the walls of which were painted red. A cubicle divider stood in the room's center. They passed an older man sleeping on a bed. The woman peeked around the cubicle wall. "Knock, knock," she said. "You have a visitor."

Matt stepped beside her and saw Mike lying propped on the bed with his leg in a cast. "Hi, Mike."

The woman backed away and Mike smiled; he looked healthy despite the bruises and cast. "Hey, Chaz."

"Janet, the woman who doesn't like people—you know, the lady who's on the square from time to time . . . ?" Mike nodded. "She heard that you were here." Matt dragged the vinyl yellow chair up to the bed and settled in. He told his story and looked at the floor, fumbling with the coat in his hands. "I'm not telling you what to do," he said. "I'm not even suggesting it, but . . ." Mike listened, watching his face, and Matt shuffled from foot to foot. "I was wondering if you'd be up for a road trip?"

Erin picked her things up at my house after work. She and her mother were coordinating their schedules for now and taking care of Gabe. "Once I have money saved, I'll need to move back into town," she said. "To be closer to work."

"Call me when you're ready and I'll help you find something," I said. I helped her pack her things into a box and suitcase. "So, Robert Layton tells me you're sweet on someone downtown."

Her mouth fell open. She threw a pair of jeans into the suitcase. "What! No. He was standing there when this guy just—"

"Swept you off your feet," Miriam finished.

"No! No, he ran into me, and—"

"Birds tweeted, rockets launched, the earth moved?" I laughed at Miriam and Erin dumped a drawer full of socks and underwear into the suitcase.

"He wouldn't want a girl with a baby," Erin said. "Trust me."

"I've been studying and watching and performing for people my whole life," Miriam said. "I can sense when someone is angry or bored."

"Are you sensing anything now?" I asked, winking at Erin.

Miriam held up her hand. "Gloria, please. I can tell if someone is anxious or worried. And I can see when someone is in love."

"Me!" Erin screamed. "I am not!"

Miriam and I laughed. "Just tell us this," I said. "Is he handsome?"

Erin zipped up the suitcase and pulled it off the bed. "Yes," she said, brushing past me.

"I knew it," Miriam said, running after her. "And what is the handsome man's name?"

Whiskers bolted from the stair landing when he heard us coming. "I don't know his name and as soon as he discovers that there are two of us in this family I doubt he'll want to know my name, either."

"Oh, a doubter," I said, loading the box into the trunk.

"And a skeptic," Miriam said, watching Erin. "But I know people, and this one is in looove." She dragged the word out and Erin slammed the trunk shut.

She turned and hugged us, and I was certain that I saw a tear in Miriam's eye. "Thank you, Gloria. Thank you both for everything," Erin said.

"Come back anytime," I said. "Bring your boyfriend. I'll leave the light on for you." She laughed and backed out of the driveway, waving. We watched her drive away and I sighed. "I hate good-byes and endings, and the conclusion of things in general."

"You'd think we'd be used to them by now," Miriam said.

I walked up the stairs to the porch. "I know. But they still stink."

Miriam picked up a large box filled with plates, saucepans, and utensils, and carried it into the house. I followed her into the garage with a huge bag of clothes. "We really need a permanent place for all this stuff," she said.

I dropped the bag. "We?"

She unloaded the box onto the shelves. "You! Dalton and Heddy and you! Who do you think I mean?"

I sorted through the clothes and laughed.

Matt's siblings all had plans to be with their in-laws on Christmas but they rearranged their plans so they could come to my house. Miriam and I shifted into high gear. There would be twenty of us, including Dalton and Heddy and Carla and Donovan, and there was lots of baking and cooking and shopping to be done.

Matthew was awkward around his brothers and sister—they were strangers, really—but that would change over the course of time. On Christmas day my grandchildren littered the living room with wrapping paper and kept Miriam on her toes. "Throw that in here," she said to each child as he or she unwrapped a gift. "No, no, not on the floor. We're not rats!"

My grandson brought his toy horse named Pink, and Whiskers spent the day darting from one hiding place to the next. Miriam said she'd never seen anything like it, and actually felt sorry for Whiskers. "There. It's passed now," she said, running through the house waving Pink in the air.

Donovan was shocked to see that not only did Santa deliver presents under his Christmas bush, but that there were presents for him at my house as well. "How'd he do that?" he screamed, opening a small plastic case filled with dinosaurs. Carla opened a package of press-on nails and Donovan yelled out, "I told Santa you wanted those!" Carla's shoulders bounced when she laughed, and I hoped that this time she could get her feet on the ground for good.

Andrew handed Matt a small box wrapped with green foil paper and a velvet ribbon. Matthew slid the bow off the box, ripped back the paper, and lifted the lid. He picked up the red spiral notebook and looked at me. "I figured you'd want it back now," I said. I watched Matt's eyes scan one page and then another of the notebook. "Take it in small bites," I whispered.

After the presents were opened, the doorbell rang and I maneuvered through the debris to the door. I threw the door open when I saw who it was. "I'm so glad you could come," I said, taking Gabe from Erin's arms.

"Since Mom's working, I knew we'd be awfully lonely today," she said.

I pressed Gabriel to my cheek and walked with him into the kitchen. "Come meet Matt."

Matt was cutting another piece of coffee cake, and glanced up to see me with the baby. "Who's this?" he said, licking his fingers.

"This is little Gabe. Miriam and I practically delivered him ourselves. And this is . . ." I turned to see Erin. "Where'd she go?" I covered Gabe's ears and yelled over his head. "Erin!"

She and Miriam walked into the kitchen and Matt's eyes beamed when he saw her. Erin blushed but I was too occupied with Gabe to notice. "This is my son Matthew," I said, pulling his face to me for a kiss. "And this is Erin. The gal we told you—"

"Hi," Matt said, smiling. He offered her a piece of coffee cake. "I won't knock that out of your hands."

She laughed and took the cake and a cup of coffee from him. He led her into the living room and I hovered in the doorway, watching them. Miriam stood at my side with her hand on Gabriel's head.

"Am I missing something?" I asked.

"Yes," she said. "But that's beside the point. I knew all along that he was the handsome young man she met downtown."

I snapped my head to look at her. "Do you think?"

She leaned over and kissed Gabe's face. "I don't know. But it would make a lovely story for their grandchildren."

After the dinner dishes were washed and put away and the children were testing their new toys, I saw the envelope in the branches and crossed over boxes and books and tiny bodies to the tree. "Merry Christmas, Walt," I whispered. I caught Matt looking at me and took the envelope off the tree for good, smiling.

EPILOGUE

So long as we love we serve;
So long as we are loved by others,
I would almost say that we are indispensable;
And no man is useless while he has a friend.
—Robert Louis Stevenson

I watch Jack work on the car and pour coffee into an insulated mug. He must be freezing out there, I think. I stick a sweet roll or, as Miriam calls it, a *heart attack shaped like a bun* in the toaster oven and wait for the icing to melt. Jack has never charged me a penny for the work he does on the cars that end up in my driveway, but he has always expected one of my sweet rolls and a cup of coffee.

Matt reaches for a pair of jeans and pulls on a worn flannel shirt. A thud at the door distracts him. The paperboy has delivered Matt's neighbor's paper to him again. He throws on his coat and walks over the small yard to the Kelseys'. Frank Kelsey answers the door in a pair of reindeer boxer shorts, his graying comb-over flapping atop his head in the morning breeze. The smell of sausage drifts out the door. Despite the time of day the Kelseys' home always smells like sausage. "I stood right there at the window and watched him throw it to your door," Frank says, taking the paper from Matt. "He knows what he's doing."

When his six-month lease ran out Matt moved across the street to the duplex next to Frank and Luanne Kelsey. Two months after they met Matt, the Kelseys took down the Christmas lights that had been up for fourteen months. Matthew helped Frank that day, and they worked together in the silence. Frank and Luanne still hope for the return of their son and weep at the not-knowing. That's the part that kills them. I know.

Mrs. Kelsey walks from the bedroom wearing a green-and-red-striped housecoat that she's snapping up to her neck. Her dyed auburn hair looks like a cinnamon bun on top of her head. "Good morning, doll," she growls as she ushers Matt inside. She sounds like a three-pack-a-day smoker but she's never lit up a day in her life. Matt normally wouldn't like someone calling him "doll," but it works with a voice like Luanne Kelsey's. "You look so handsome today," she adds. She pulls glasses from her pocket and perches them on the end of her nose as she fixes the collar on his shirt. The scent of Jean Naté fills the space around them as she finishes. "What a great day this will be." She holds his chin in her hand. "Do you want breakfast?"

"Can't today." He looks at Frank in his boxer shorts. "Are you going like that?"

The phone rings and I answer it, nibbling on my second sweet roll of the morning. "Do you have your work clothes on?" Matt asks.

"Always," I say, taking another bite. "Good meeting this morning?"

"Real good. I just dropped Frank off."

I believe God put Frank Kelsey beside Matt that first day at AA. Matthew has been able to tell things to Frank that he's not ready to talk with me about. Frank knows what it's like to be broken, and has been a good friend to him.

It wasn't an easy year for Matt; he had plenty of setbacks and failures, but they didn't hobble him.

Matt says that in a lot of ways it feels like he's crawled back from the dead. With each passing day he has come back to life, and I'm proud. Very proud.

"I figured you'd be gone by now," Matt says.

I look out the window at Jack in the driveway. "Unless you pick me up, I can't go anywhere until Jack finishes with my car."

"What's wrong with your car?"

"I have no idea. Jack pulled in today to help with the Gray Goose that was left here three days ago, but said he also noticed a leak under my car. He's got both hoods up and tools spread out everywhere."

"I'll come get you," Matt says.

I reach for my cleaning supplies out of the utility closet and put them in a box. Five months ago Dalton saw a building on a street past Wilson's that was for sale. "It'd be perfect for your work," he said. "You could use it for all your classes and use it as a distribution center for all your stuff." It wasn't a possibility for so many reasons. "There are donors," Dalton said. He turned the corners of his mouth up in a grin and I knew he and Heddy had been busy. "Miriam, too," he said, winking at her.

The old brick building had once been a small warehouse. It needed a lot of work before we could use it—some windows needed to be replaced, the roof needed patching up, the plumbing needed to be updated, walls needed to be erected, and every square inch of the inside needed to be painted, including the concrete floor. We've been scrubbing and cleaning for the last four weeks, with little to show for it, but we do what we can—even Miriam, who always wears bright yellow latex gloves, her "green wellies,"and a blue work jumpsuit. Matt calls it her HazMat suit. "Hazardous materials coming through!" he yells whenever she passes. At the pace we're able to work, I can't imagine when we'll ever be able to actually use the building.

Miriam's house turned out better than she imagined. She was with me for ten weeks in all, refusing to move back in until every screw, tile, and picture was in place. She tells me that I should move in with her and redo my place, but I don't think Whiskers and I are ready for that again. For the first time since I've known her, Miriam has decorated the outside of her house for Christmas. Dalton volunteered to help but soon regretted it when Miriam barked orders up to him on the ladder. He endured, and her house looks lovely. I opted for my usual evergreen and lights wrapped around my porch. I know it's simple but I've

never been much of a decorator. I leave that to
Miriam.

Matt honks the horn and I jump. "Good grief! I
just hung up the phone," I say, pulling on my yellow
boots. One pant leg gets stuck on the top of the boot
and I stomp my foot, hoping it will fall as I reach for
the cleaning supplies. The pant sticks to the top of the
boot, but I ignore it and run out the door. Jack Andrews is gone; I hadn't even heard him leave.

"You got here fast," I say.

"I was around the corner," he says. "Where's
Miriam?"

"I don't know. We were supposed to take our walk
and have breakfast, but she's not home."

"Getting her hair colored?"

I laugh. "Could be! The world stops on a dime
when that appointment rolls around. Do you have
class today?" He shakes his head. Matt got his GED
and takes classes at college while he works at Wilson's. He's no longer in security, but instead works as
a sales associate. He's the most knowledgeable on the
staff, if you ask me. Carla still works on the janitorial
team, but only during the day, while Donovan goes to
school.

Matt met a girl with whom he fell in love the first

time he saw her. He learned her name at my house and will marry her in April. Erin's mother found a job here and moved into town nine months ago; Erin and Gabe moved in with her. While Lois and Erin plan the wedding, Miriam and I play with Gabe—my eighth grandchild—and watch him grow. I swear he calls me Grandma, but Miriam says I'm "barking mad." Regardless, Gabe is a brilliant and beautiful baby.

Mike was never far from Matthew's mind, and when he was able to travel, Matt drove him south to Alabama. As he pulled into a home's driveway a woman was standing, waiting at the door. She began to scream when she saw the car, and in moments the driveway was full of people laughing, crying, and jumping. Mike stepped slowly out of the car and his parents enveloped him in tears. No one in the crowd moved or attempted to break the small huddle of humanity. Matt said it was one of the most rewarding things he'd ever done in his life.

As Matt drives through town, I admire the decorated fir trees in the square and the decorations in all the store windows. I can't believe it's already Christmas again! I watch Janet wander through the town square, and wave at her. I used to think that I had to do everything within my ability to bring someone to a place of change, but I've finally learned, like Heddy says, that's not my job. I must say, I sleep better at night now. We pull into the parking lot of the building and the gravel crunches beneath the tires. A banner stretches across the doorway and I shriek when I read it: GLORY'S PLACE.

"Who put that up?" I ask.

Matt smiles and lifts the cleaning supplies out of the trunk. "I did. It's not permanent, but I thought people should know you're here."

I stand looking at the bright green-and-red sign. "Glory's Place? I didn't think I'd put my name on it."

He moves me toward the front door. "We love it."

"You and who else?" I ask.

He opens the door and cheers erupt throughout the building. "We do," he says, screaming into my ear. I grope for the bobby pin on the back of my head.

"It's too late for that now," Miriam says, linking her arm through mine.

I look across the floor at a sea of people. Robert and Kate Layton and Jack Andrews are here. "I was told to keep you at your house until Matt called," Jack says, yelling above the noise. Dalton and Heddy are here; and there's Carla, Erin, and Lois, who's holding Gabe; lots of friends from church; and Frank and Luanne

Kelsey. Marshall Wilson waves at me. I recognize one face after another. My three oldest children walk out from behind huge heating boxes, and I scream when I see them. As Andrew, Daniel, and Stephanie stand beside me, tears fill my eyes.

"This is the work crew," Matt says, leaning into my ear. "We're building walls, putting in bathrooms and a kitchen, and will have this place opened in a few weeks instead of months."

Robert Layton steps in beside me and waves his arms in the air. The crowd quiets and I can feel my heart in my ears. "I've known Gloria for several years, and for all that time I've asked her when she's ever going to open a place for her work. And for several years she has ignored me. If you know Gloria, you know that's not unusual." The crowd laughs and I shake my head, wiping my eyes. "Gloria, once and for all, would you please clean out your garage?" I nod, laughing, and use my palms to wipe away the stream of tears on my face.

Matt stands on his toes and cups his hand around his mouth. "All right, everybody. Man your battle stations and let's get to work." The crowd claps and disperses to every corner of the building.

Miriam wraps her arm around me, squeezing my

shoulder. "Is it better than you ever imagined?" she asks.

I smile as I watch Matt and a group of men haul in a load of lumber and supplies. "Yes," I say, trying to find my voice.

Art Lender sneaks in beside me and gives me a hug. "Thank you for everything, Miss Glory." He looks at Miriam and tips his ball cap. "Thank you, Miss Mary," he says, walking past us.

"Am," Miriam says, yelling after him. "Miriam." I laugh and she smacks her hands together. "I refuse to be called Miss Mary!" I laugh harder and she shakes her head, grumbling. "Oh, forget it." She runs to help Heddy and Dalton rip up some floorboards and I spin, looking around me. Where is a camera when I need it? Some would say that my friendship with Miriam has drawn her out of herself, but I don't know if that's entirely true. I believe our friendship has made us both better, as any good friendship should do.

I look around the room and try to take it all in. In the past year I have gotten to know both the stranger who lived beside me and the stranger who knocked on my door. I never expected any of it. Neither did they. Matt told me that he used to look at his life and think, *How did I get here?* Today he says, "How did I come this far?" For years he stumbled and wandered, getting bloodied and bruised around every bend. He had lost his way, and his vision was nearly gone, but grace was relentless, always inviting him to come Home. That's why grace came down at Christmas, to love and pursue us through dark days and desperate nights. Try as we might, we can't outrun it.

I pick Gabe up and press his little face close to mine. "There's your daddy," I say, pointing to Matthew. "There's your daddy." Gabe looks nothing like Matthew, but neither he nor Matt seems to know that. Matt waves at the baby and Gabe kicks his chubby legs and claps his hands together. I smile and kiss his face.

Like Walt said years ago . . . life always makes a way.

Don't Miss Donna VanLiere's Wonderful New Novel

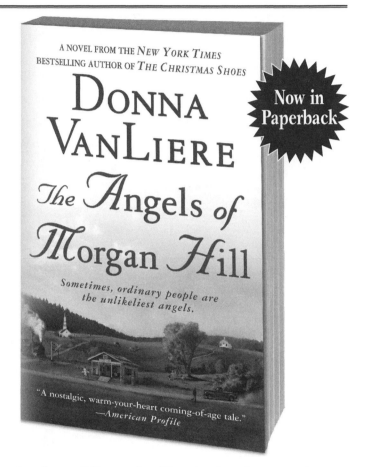

A NOVEL FROM THE *NEW YORK TIMES* BESTSELLING AUTHOR OF *THE CHRISTMAS SHOES*

DONNA VANLIERE

The Angels of Morgan Hill

Sometimes, ordinary people are the unlikeliest angels.

"A nostalgic, warm-your-heart coming-of-age tale."
—*American Profile*

Now in Paperback

A tale of two different families sharing the mysteries of faith and the hope of belonging.

AVAILABLE NOW ON DVD

The Sequel to the Heart-Warming Hit,
THE CHRISTMAS SHOES

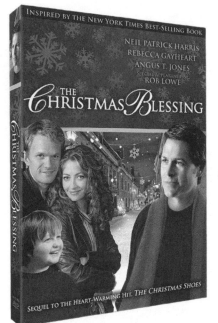

Golden Globe® nominee
NEIL PATRICK HARRIS

REBECCA GAYHEART

ANGUS T. JONES

And a special appearance by
ROB LOWE

Based on the *New York Times* bestselling book

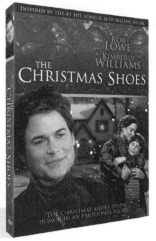

And Don't Miss
THE CHRISTMAS SHOES

Available Wherever DVDs Are Sold